South of the Badlands

Rancher Dan Johnson had lost everything in the previous six-months: his wife and children to a mysterious fever and most of his stock to a ceaseless drought. Now the bank was threatening to take the little he had left.

All seemed lost until Rafe Jarrow and his gang held up the stagecoach carrying a shipment of bullion for Cooper's Plain, a town perched on the edge of a vast salt flats desert.

Now the banker offers to clear Johnson's debts if he can get the bullion back, so Dan heads out after Jarrow and his infamous outfit. But are his gun skills good enough?

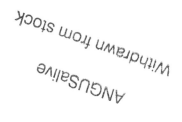

South of the Badlands

MICHAEL D. GEORGE

A Black Horse Western

ROBERT HALE · LONDON

ISBN 0 7090 7304 6

Robert Hale Limited
Clerkenwell House
Clerkenwell Green
London EC1R 0HT

Typeset by
Derek Doyle & Associates, Liverpool.
Printed and bound in Great Britain by
Antony Rowe Limited, Wiltshire

Dedicated with gratitude and respect
to my friend, Roy Edward Disney.
A truly nice man.

ONE

Some men are made of granite and some of sand. The strong can withstand anything that fate throws against them whilst the weak tend to simply perish. This is how things are and have always been, for the most part. But even those men who seem invulnerable can be brought to their knees when they believe that the elements or God have forsaken them.

What can an ordinary man do when he finds that everything he has loved, cherished and held dear, suddenly evaporates into a heartbreaking heat haze? During the previous six months Dan Johnson's life had completely altered until he no longer seemed to recognize even his own reflection in his wall mirror.

The house that he had built was now empty. Only his sad voice echoed around its walls where once there had been so many other happy voices.

Would he awake from the devilish nightmare and find everything restored to normality or had it all just been an illusion in a mind that had broken? Nothing made any sense any longer but at least the pain was gone, leaving just numbness in the place that had once been occupied by his heart. Reluctantly he faced reality with the same grim determination that had brought him to this harsh land so long ago when he had still regarded himself as young.

If he had known then what awaited him, he might have taken a safer route to this point in his life. But men did not get a second chance in this or any other life, he knew that.

A man can only stand so much before even the strongest snaps like a weathered branch. Dan Johnson had withstood more than most but even he knew that he was no longer the man that he had once been all those years before.

Johnson was just the empty shell of that creature. Nothing more than shadow of his former self.

How could he be anything else?

It had been a cruel, heartless summer in this desolate and unforgiving land, but at first it had not been the weather which had tortured the clean-living rancher. That had only added to the pain which had nearly destroyed his mind.

The rancher stared at the windswept hill behind his ranch house and swallowed hard as his eyes focused on the white marker stones that reflected the harsh hot sun. Every one of his beloved family was buried on that hill.

His wife Ellie, daughters Vera and Samantha and his sons Rufas and John. They were all there lying next to one another. He had dug each of their graves and laid them all to rest with his own hands. At first he had read words from the family Bible, but by the time he had buried the last of them, he had lost all faith in everything he had once held dear.

The doctor had said it was a fever of sorts but nobody really knew the truth. All anyone knew for certain was that it killed with a viciousness and speed that chilled even hardened men of the range. The rancher wondered how anything so evil could have found his family out here in the wilderness.

Dan Johnson had not even felt ill during the six weeks it had taken to wipe out his entire family. He wondered why he alone of all of them had survived the curse.

But he had. Maybe it was because his life had not been as pure as theirs and he was not as welcome in heaven as they were. Perhaps he himself had been the truly cursed one. To lose a strong young wife was unexpected enough, but to lose innocent children had been more than he had been able to justify.

Although not a religious man himself, Johnson had always ensured that his family went to the small church in Cooper's Plain every Sunday morning. Always managed to find a few coins for them to put on the collection plate.

But that had been then. Now he had no room for those who spouted from their beloved Good Book. He raged at anyone who even tried to reason with his loss. For many months, as far as he was concerned, death could not come to him fast enough.

God had betrayed and rejected him.

Stolen everything that had made his life worth living and repaid him with a drought that now started to destroy what was left of his stock.

Why?

It was a simple enough question but impossible to answer.

Johnson leaned on the top pole of the corral and gazed at the dust blowing away what had once been fertile top soil. Now even the oldest of trees with the deepest roots seemed to be suffering beneath the hot sun. Yet he knew that soon the rain would come as it always did and within a few short weeks the place would be green again.

But there were no clouds in the sky.

Where was the rain this year? Where were those precious clouds?

Dried and withered by the harsh climate, his ranch was now facing certain death. The grass had already died and even the sagebrush offered little nourishment to his once prime herd of white-faced cattle.

Wind swept across the jagged spires that edged the entire horizon from where the rancher stood. Dan Johnson had never known the elements to be so hostile. Half his stock had already died of hunger and what was left needed vital supplies which he no longer had the funds to obtain.

Johnson knew that he should have acted sooner but after burying his last child, he had simply lost track of everything including the condition of the animals which had relied upon him to care for them.

Maybe he had thought that he too would be taken

by the fever which had destroyed his family and could see no point in even bothering to care for livestock which would probably outlive him anyway. It might have been that he simply could not face the cruel ride over the harsh land that separated his meagre cattle spread from Cooper's Plain.

Water was still plentiful in the streams that ran through the rocky ground but nothing can survive totally on water.

Dan Johnson had awoken this day with a hunger in his belly that told him that whatever else had happened in the last six months, he was still alive.

However much he despised himself for being so, he still lived.

The rancher had walked out into the blazing morning sun and decided that he had to try and get some money to tide him over until the rain visited his remote land once again. Once the rain came, the grass would grow and the cattle fatten up.

That was the way it always worked, but Johnson knew that this year, things had not been normal. He had borrowed money to pay the medical bills when his family had first fallen victim to the strange fever.

The doctor had made a tidy sum but none of his medicines had worked. Johnson knew that he had paid willingly, thinking, as most people do, that doctors can cure anything. The truth is far more cruel. For they are only men and men can and do make mistakes.

Normally by this time of the year, Johnson would have cleared his debts and started to show a little profit.

But Johnson knew that this was anything but an average year for him. He had borrowed more money for feed when his family were still only sick.

Now he knew that he had to try and get more, but there was only one place in Cooper's Plain that lent money and that was the bank. Johnson surmised that he had probably exhausted that avenue of credit, but still had to try.

The forty-three year old man had aged far beyond his years of late but the thin black gelding recognized its master as he dragged his saddle gear off the bleached fencing and approached it.

Johnson knew that he had to ride to town and attempt to get that vital loan. The odds were stacked against him but without it, what was left of his stock would die before the rains came.

The strong arms that had never failed him in all his years placed the worn saddle on top of the blanket, then he did up the cinch straps.

He mounted the animal and rode slowly from the corral, heading for Cooper's Plain. He had no gun or rifle nor any other things of value left.

Everything of value had long gone.

TWO

The six riders hauled in their reins and studied the terrain which stretched out below them. If anywhere resembled the desolate landscape of another world, this was it. There seemed to be nothing in the maze of rocky canyons, only dust which drifted off the surface of the craggy spires, driven by the relentless hot breeze which taunted their trail-weary eyes.

This was a place where death ruled unchallenged. Nothing lived down there except sidewinders and flesh-stripping ants. The only sign of life came from above the heads of the horsemen. Black shadows traced out across the almost white rocks that were littered around them. The riders peered up and felt uneasy as they looked at the massive birds who only survived when other animals or people died. The vultures circled them on the warm thermals, as if knowing what fate had in store for the half-dozen riders, a little further down the trail.

But these men acknowledged nothing except the stagecoach that wound its way through the narrow

13

canyon. The clouds of billowing dust had risen from the wheels of the stage against the blue horizon long before any of the riders had actually seen the team of six horses pulling the weathered vehicle.

There was only one way though this mountain range and the Overland Stage was taking it as it had done countless times before over the years. For the driver and his shotgun guard it was just another day when they had to spend twelve straight hours carrying passengers and goods from one place to another.

The six men refreshed themselves with water from their canteens knowing that they only had to remain exactly where they were and their victims would come straight to them.

They were the spiders and they had woven their web.

Rafe Jarrow had led his younger followers for more than two long years and honed their skills until they were sharper than a straight razor. Each were expert shots and few could handle horseflesh as well as they could.

They had been trained by a master who deserved the $10,000 reward money on his head. He had come up the hard way and done his apprenticeship with gangs like the infamous Youngers and Daltons. They had taught him well.

What Jarrow did not know about robbing stage-coaches could be etched on the head of a pin. It simply did not exist. He had graduated from being the rider who risked his neck and transferred from the saddle of a galloping horse on to the side of a thundering stagecoach into the man who gave the orders.

Orders which were obeyed.

For two years the outlaws had roamed unchecked in and out of the notorious badlands harvesting the strongboxes found on the stagecoaches which travelled virtually unprotected from one isolated Texan town to another.

They had made a lot of money and managed to spend every cent of it in the badlands, a place where the law had yet to strangle with its grip of respectability.

Jarrow's band of young outlaws were good at what they did and yet few knew the names of those who rode with the famed outlaw. His shadow was big enough to envelop them all. They were known as the Jarrow Gang or simply the Outfit.

Apart from Rafe Jarrow himself, who was a shade over thirty, none of the men who sat astride their horses was even close to being twenty-one. But it was not years that made them what they were, it was the training that they had received from the ruthless outlaw. Jarrow had discovered long ago that it was far easier to mould youngsters into what you wanted them to be, than trust older men who had become set in their ways.

Rafe Jarrow glanced across through the cigarette smoke that drifted between his teeth at the smiling faces of his eager troop. Joey Franks and Curly Potter had been with him the longest and he trusted them with his life. They were loyal. Lon Talpin and Red

Clyde had been troublesome youngsters when he had first enlisted them into his select band and were now second only to himself with their lethal weaponry. Their loyalty had yet to be tested. The last of his outfit to join him was Neddy Holmes. He seemed younger than any of them but looks could be deceptive. He could outdraw even Jarrow himself, yet his accuracy was often lacking. They had proved themselves a score of times and that counted for something with Rafe Jarrow.

The older rider nodded at them. They all looked excited.

He had brought his men down from the badlands because he had been told that the pickings were far richer in the Lone Star State. That had been so for the most part. Then Jarrow had continued further and further south until they reached this strange desolate land.

It did not match the description that Jarrow had been given about it. Yet all the town names were correct. A less confident soul might have taken this as an omen and returned back to the safety of the badlands. But Rafe Jarrow never changed his plans simply because there was dust instead of grass beneath the hoofs of his horse.

What he did not know was that they had come at the wrong time of year for it to match the tales of a fertile green country where the cattle were fat and the bankers even fatter. But as he stood in his stirrups and saw the stagecoach heading closer and closer towards them, he cared little for details. All he knew

16

for certain was that he had found the correct road leading through the canyons.

'I thought you told us that there was knee-high grass here, Rafe?' Franks asked the rider.

'There ought to be,' Jarrow replied, tossing the butt of his cigarette away.

'Knee-high dust, more like.' Red Clyde spat.

But Jarrow cared nothing for landscapes. He barely noticed the difference between a green pasture and a baked plain. All he saw was the trail ahead.

A trail that led to his next conquest.

The six riders screwed the stoppers back on to their canteens and hung them back on their saddle horns. Then they pulled their bandannas up over their noses and tightened the draw-strings on their Stetsons under their chins.

They were ready.

It was nearly two in the afternoon by the golden hunter watch in Rafe Jarrow's gloved hand. This had to be the badly named noon stage that was heading for Cooper's Plain, he figured. His cold calculating eyes watched the stage getting closer and closer to where they lay in wait. Once every week the stage carried a strongbox full of golden eagles from the bank at Smith's Spring to the one in Cooper's Plain. Jarrow had paid well for that juicy titbit of information and was now ready to get a return on his investment.

'Come on, boys.' Jarrow sank his spurs into the flesh of his horse and led the riders to the tall rocks that edged the dusty trail road.

If nature had designed a place that was perfect for an ambush then this had to be it, Jarrow thought as he controlled his horse and squinted through the rocks at the approaching coach.

The six riders drew their guns with one hand as they steadied their horses with the other.

Like rolling thunder, the sound of the metal-rimmed wheels of the stage echoed off the canyon walls all about them. It felt like an eternity to the horsemen who were ready and able to do the job at which they had become experts. Yet for all their experience, they still found the seconds before they struck out at their unsuspecting victims nerve-racking.

Suddenly the stagecoach rolled past where the riders were hiding.

Each man turned his horse.

They had seen the white hair of the bearded driver flowing behind his jacket collar and the half-asleep guard at his side.

With an alarming turn of speed, the half-dozen riders drove their well tutored mounts after the stage. Rafe Jarrow waved his gun barrel at his gang and they fanned out to either side of the unsuspecting vehicle as he himself trailed the rocking coach. Neither man atop the high driver's seat of the Overland Stage had any idea that they were now being followed.

Even if they had known, there was nothing that they could have done about it on this road. This was

18

not a place where a six-horse team could be given its head and allowed to gallop away from anything. This road demanded a coach-driver to be accurate with his heavy reins as he steered the powerful horses through the twisting rocks.

Rafe Jarrow watched as two of his men rode alongside the vehicle and stretched out for the high roof-bars of the stagecoach.

THREE

Joey Franks and Curly Potter leapt from their saddles and caught hold of the metal luggage-rail that encircled the top of the thundering vehicle. Dismissing the three passengers as not being any threat, the two outlaws clung to the sides of the rocking vehicle and hauled themselves up either side of the stagecoach until they reached the roof.

The pair steadied themselves as they had done a dozen times before and moved over the stagecoach roof through the tied-down bags. Both men drew their weapons and trained them on the heads of the unsuspecting driver and guard.

Joey Franks smashed the barrel of his pistol across the side of the guard's head. Blood erupted from the deep gash sending the limp body falling from the fast-moving vehicle. It disappeared into the clouds of dust that billowed up from the hoofs of the six-horse team.

Franks clambered down next to the startled driver as the man's head turned, his eyes staring straight down the long barrel of the Colt Peacemaker.

'Rein in, old-timer,' Franks screamed out at the frightened man. The driver did not have to be told twice. His right boot was thrust on to the brake pole and the wiry arms hauled back on the heavy leather reins. The lead horse began to slow and the entire team of matched animals followed suit.

Just after the weathered old stagecoach came to a halt, the terrified screams of its only female passenger rang out through the dusty canyon.

A triumphant Curly Potter stood on the roof and walked to the side of Franks who was already hauling the heavy metal strongbox from beneath the driver's seat. Both men lifted it and then dropped it over the side of the high seat, down to the ground.

'You armed?' Potter asked the old man who was shaking as he tried to hold on to the reins.

'Nope. Never carry a weapon. Guns kinda explode in my holsters. Had to quit wearing the things.' The white-haired man was scared and it showed. 'Blewed a toe off back in seventy-six.'

Curly Potter pulled the driver's heavy coat apart and checked anyway. There was no sign of any weapons on the skinny frame.

'Stay here and keep your foot on that brake pole.'

The driver nodded.

Franks climbed down from the driver's box and watched as the other riders gathered around him. Rafe Jarrow had caught the reins of both horses when his men had jumped from their saddles on to the fast-moving coach.

'How's the guard?' Franks asked wondering if he had hit the man too hard before he fell helplessly from the speeding vehicle.

'Dead,' Red Clyde said with a twisted smile on his lips.

'Did he land badly?' Franks wanted more information.

'Bad enough.' Clyde added. 'Mind you, having my mare run over his head didn't help his cause none.'

Several of the outlaws laughed. They had killed their fair share of shotgun guards over the years. One more meant little to any of them.

Rafe Jarrow dismounted and stared into the stage-coach at the three shocked passengers: two fat men and a handsome female in her thirties. The female had managed to stop screaming by forcing a black lace handkerchief into her face. Yet her eyes still flashed in total fear.

The outlaw leader cocked the hammer of his pistol, then turned the door-handle of the coach and pulled it open.

'Get out, folks,' he ordered.

Reluctantly, the three people climbed down from the coach's interior into the blazing sunshine and stood close together. They were staring hard with a mixture of curiosity and trepidation at the men who wore their bandannas over their faces.

Jarrow poked the barrel of his Colt into the fat bellies of the two men in their tailored suits and nodded knowingly.

'Looks like we have two wealthy ones here, boys,'

23

Jarrow observed loudly. 'Fat bellies means fat wallets.'

'You don't want us. You have the strongbox,' the fatter of the men said in a voice which tried hard to sound confident yet somehow failed.

Jarrow stepped closer to the man and looked hard at him.

'Are you anything to do with the bank that owns that box, mister?' he asked curiously.

The man began to sweat. It came suddenly from beneath the band of his hat and trickled over his pink cheeks.

'Why do you ask me that?'

Jarrow pressed the barrel of his gun against the rotund man's fleshy left jowl.

'Most men have some colour in their faces but you are as pink as the day you crawled out from between your mother's legs. I figure that only two kinds of men have skin that never sees the sun. Men who earn their living as gamblers and men who spend their entire life inside a bank counting money. You ain't dressed like no gambler.'

'A flawed deduction, sir.' The man coughed as his eyes darted to the other two page passengers and then back to the outlaws. 'I could be the owner of a general store or something similar.'

'Show me your hands,' Rafe Jarrow demanded.

Reluctantly the man did so.

Jarrow grabbed one of the hands and raised it high enough for even his mounted men to see clearly.

'Soft like a baby's bottom. This dude ain't never

worked in no store, not with hands like this. So I'll ask you again, have you anything to do with this strongbox?'

The man refused to speak. He just stared at the gun aimed straight at his face.

'He ain't worth killing,' Neddy Holmes remarked. He got down from his horse and approached the nervous female. She was at least five inches taller than the young outlaw but that did not put him off. 'Howdy, ma'am.'

The woman was dressed in a way most females of her age and class dressed. The black clothes were tailored and covered every part of her still-slim body. Only her face remained uncovered and dotted with beads of sweat.

'I like the smell of a woman whose in her prime,' Neddy said. He inhaled her distinctive perfume and began to stroke her shoulder with his left index finger. 'I bet you taste almost as good as you look.'

She said nothing but watched as his finger became more and more adventurous.

Curly stared down at Jarrow from the driver's seat.

'Shall I leave this old guard or kill him?'

Jarrow glanced up. 'Tie his hands. These folks will need him when we've gone. I reckon none of them can handle a team of horses.'

'OK!' Curly touched the wide brim of his Stetson.

The second fat man stepped away from the coach until he was nose to nose with Neddy Holmes.

'I suggest you leave this lady alone, you filthy young buck.'

'You are worth killing, fatmouth.' Without a second thought, Neddy raised his gun and squeezed its trigger. The single shot at close range took half the man's head off. Blood and chunks of brain tissue covered the screaming female a fraction of a second before she fainted next to the crumpled corpse.

'Can I tend her?' Neddy asked Jarrow.

The leader of the gang nodded. 'Be quick.'

Rafe Jarrow leaned a hand against the chest of the other fat man and watched as Neddy scooped the female up from the ground and carried her around the coach.

'I protest, sir,' the sweating man managed to say.

The eyes of the outlaw leader and the man met.

'I like a man who has grit. I was gonna kill you but now I'll just split your skull open a tad to let some fresh air into it.'

The sound of the woman's clothing being stripped from her unconscious body filled their ears. Then they heard Neddy grunting. It lasted only a few seconds before he returned to the rest of the gathering doing up the buttons on his baggy pants.

'You done?' Jarrow asked.

Neddy Holmes nodded. 'Yep. She was real sweet.'

'One day you ought to try a woman who ain't unconscious,' Franks said knowingly.

Rafe Jarrow swiftly snapped the barrel of his gun against the sweating fat man's head and then turned to the strongbox behind him. He fired and took the padlock clean off before the man had fallen to the ground. Lon Talpin slid from his mount and pulled the lid open. They all stared at the fresh-minted golden coins.

'Fill your saddle-bags, boys,' Rafe Jarrow said, gripping his saddle horn. He stepped into his stirrup and hauled himself up on top of his mount. 'There's a town called Cooper's Plain about ten miles due west of here and I'm thirsty.'

Curly Potter tied the last knot in the rawhide bindings around the ancient wrists of the stagecoach driver. The old driver just sat with his foot on the long brake pole and knew that he would have little help to release the tight rawhide.

'Come on,' Jarrow called up at the young outlaw.

'We through?' Curly asked. He climbed down from the high driver's perch and stepped on to the back of his waiting horse.

Jarrow pulled his reins hard to his left and spurred his loyal horse.

'We're through. Come on, boys.'

The five riders galloped after their leader. As they drove their mounts in the direction of Cooper's Plain, none of them had noticed the figure high up in the rocky crags. Everything they had done during the last five minutes had been witnessed by Dan Johnson who stood next to his lathered-up horse.

Johnson mounted the animal and began to descend slowly towards the trail road.

FOUR

At first, the old stagecoach driver had thought that one of the outlaws had returned to finish him off and those who were left of his passengers. Then his old eyes had noted that this was no outlaw, he was just an ordinary man whose poverty showed in his worn cothing and thin features. This rider did not possess guns or even a hat. In this blazing sun the only men who did not wear hats were those who could not afford one. The price of even a cheap hat could feed a family for more than a week. This man was poor.

Dan Johnson sat silently in his saddle staring at the horrific scene before him for more than a minute. His had been an isolated existence for more years than he cared to recall and he had seen death many times, but nothing like this.

This was carnage.

There had never been anything like this happening in this part of the country since Johnson had first settled here.

It seemed unreal to the hardened eyes of the rancher.

'You gonna help us, sonny?' the stagecoach driver asked loudly.

Johnson looked up at the man with a mane of white hair and a beard to match. He did not reply. His eyes stared down at the two men lying on the ground. One was still alive but bleeding badly from the cut on his temple whilst the other did not have enough head left to be anything other than dead.

Johnson rubbed his dry mouth and then sighed heavily. He had butchered most animals in his time to put food on the table for his family but there had never been any anger in his actions, only regret.

The rancher slowly eased himself down from his tired horse and lifted up the still-dazed man until he was able to prop him against the small front wheel of the stagecoach. The wound was ugly but not life-threatening. Johnson could see that it was already starting to dry out.

The man's eyelids flickered. He tried to focus on the face of the quiet rancher who was trying to stop the bleeding by pinching the torn skin together.

'Who are you?' he asked feebly.

'Dan Johnson,' came the almost whispered reply after Johnson lifted the man's own hand to the wound and pushed it against it. 'Keep your hand there. The bleeding will stop in a while.'

'Thank you,' the man said.

The lean rancher stood, climbed up the side of the

stage and moved along the wooden seat until he reached the flustered old man.

He looked at the tight knots on the rawhide, then reached inside one of his denim pants pockets until he located his penknife. He used his fingernails to release the sharp blade from the body of the knife, Johnson carefully cut through the leather bindings until the driver's wrists were freed.

'Thank you, stranger,' the old man gasped in relief.

Johnson did not say a word. He had been alone for so long that he actually found speaking difficult. How he had managed to speak to the large man on the ground confused him. He was not a man of words. He had always relied upon his actions to get him through life.

'They call me Sagebrush. What they call you?' The driver was rubbing his wrists trying to get his blood to circulate.

'Dan Johnson.'

'Well thanks, Dan.' The man smiled with a mouth that had no teeth.

'You ain't got no teeth,' Johnson muttered. He had never seen a mouth totally empty before. 'How can you eat?'

Sagebrush pulled out a small leather bag his deep jacket-pocket and teased the draw-string. He pulled out a gleaming set of dentures.

'Ain't they the prettiest set of teeth you ever done seen?'

Johnson raised his eyebrows. He was amazed and

somewhat alarmed at the sight. He had never even heard of false teeth.

'I don't get it, Sagebrush.'

'Store-bought. El Paso.' Sagebrush put them back into the leather pouch and tightened the string. 'When I gets hungry for anything other than beans, I pops them beauties into my old mouth and eats. I could gnaw the leg off a buffalo with them.'

Johnson nodded and was about to return to his horse when he saw the female lying down in the dusty shadows of the stagecoach.

His eyes narrowed.

'A woman!'

Sagebrush wound the reins around the brake pole. 'I forgot all about her. She ain't dead is she?'

Silently Dan Johnson walked along the roof of the coach and climbed down the vehicle. He stepped on to the large rear wheel and then dropped on to the parched ground and paused. His eyes studied her with a curiosity which suddenly filled him with embarrassment when he realized that she was still breathing.

The woman was unconscious. She had to be, he thought. Her black skirt and petticoats had been hoisted up and were covering her upper body.

Johnson stepped closer to her. She had a handsome face unlike those he was used to seeing. He seldom met women like her and when he did, they usually ignored him. He cast his attention down at her exposed lower body. Her expensive undergarments had been ripped apart by fevered hands. Dan

32

Johnson felt his throat go dry and his face redden when his eyes lingered too long on that which he knew was not for his eyes.

There was something in the face that reminded the rancher of his late wife. Yet they were from different worlds. His wife had worked harder than most to make their humble existence bearable whilst this woman had probably never had to do anything for herself.

'Is she OK, Dan?' Sagebrush asked from the roof of the stagecoach.

'Yep,' Johnson replied. For the first time in six months the rancher realized that he too was still alive and still had feelings.

A shudder raced over Johnson as he bent down and pulled her skirt down to cover her up. He then straightened up and looked hard at the old man who had climbed down to the ground.

'One of them young outlaws sowed some wild oats,' the driver said, rubbing his neck.

Johnson shook his head.

'He tried to have his way with her, but I think he kinda missed, if you get my drift?'

The old man nodded slowly. 'He was the excitable type. That's why he blowed the head off that passenger.'

Dan Johnson knelt and scooped the woman off the sand, then carried her to the coach. Sagebrush opened the door and the rancher carefully sat her on one of the seats. Suddenly her eyes opened and she blinked hard.

'You'll be safe now, ma'am.' Johnson drawled. He could see that she realized that someone had interfered with her underclothing. He cleared his throat. 'One of the bandits tried to have himself some fun at your expense.'

Her face went ashen.

'Don't fret. He failed.' Johnson closed the coach door and walked back to the side of the old driver.

'You any idea who them outlaws were, Sagebrush?' Johnson heard himself ask as he wandered to the back of the stagecoach and lifted the heavy tarp.

'Nope,' Sagebrush answered. 'What you looking for?'

'You got any horse-feed?' Johnson asked. 'My mount ain't had a decent meal in months.'

The old man looked at the painfully thin horse and then reached into the rear of the coach and dragged out a sack of oats. He pointed to the sack.

'Take as much as you like, son. I owe you.'

Dan Johnson pulled the sack off the tail-gate and carried it to the exhausted horse. He poured a huge pile on to the ground and watched as it started to eat.

'Where were those varmints headed, Sagebrush?'

'I heard one of them saying that it was ten miles to Cooper's Plain,' Sagebrush answered scratching his beard thoughtfully.

'They don't seem to know their way round these parts very well, do they,' the rancher said straightening up and looking at the body.

'But it is about ten miles, Dan.'

'It is if'n you use this trail road but only half that

34

distance through the peaks.' Johnson pointed at the almost white jagged skyline.

'What you figurin' on doing?'

'Getting to Cooper's Plain before them,' Dan Johnson said bluntly.

'But why?' Sagebrush asked as he watched the tall rancher picking up the dead man and carrying his body to the rear of the stagecoach. Johnson placed the blood-soaked body on to the tail-gate and lowered the tarp.

'Somebody has got to warn the sheriff.' The rancher helped the injured man to his feet and into the coach before securing the door.

'But why you?'

'There ain't nobody else, Sagebrush.'

FIVE

Dan Johnson steered his black gelding along the narrow trail through the jagged peaks. It was a route that he had travelled countless times before in the past. He knew that time was on his side and he ought to reach Cooper's Plain at least an hour before the six outlaws arrived but he did not relax for a second. He had told Sagebrush not to bring the stagecoach into the remote town for at least two hours.

The last thing the two surviving passengers needed was to confront the six hardened outlaws. The rancher knew that if anything was going to happen, it would probably do so within the first hour of the gang's arrival in the town.

When the rider reached the highest point on the narrow trail, Johnson pulled back on his reins and stared down into the maze of canyons to his right. The road wound its way like a snake far below him. He could see the half-dozen horsemen riding slowly along its dusty trail. Johnson imagined that their saddle-bags were laden down with the loot they had stolen from the stagecoach.

Johnson continued on down the other side of the peaks. He could now see the town bathed in the merciless sunlight. There was not a hint of colour remaining anywhere in this hard cruel landscape.

Dust drifted off the jagged peaks across the town. Normally the surrounding ranch-land would have been green by this time of year, giving justification to its very existence.

Cooper's Plain was a quiet town that existed against all the odds on the very edge of a desert of pure salt. A hundred square miles of white crystals marked the boundary beyond which no sane man had ever dared to venture.

A boundary which normally would have been in marked contrast to the fertile lands that men like Dan Johnson ranched. But beneath the blazing sun everything had been bleached to the colour of bone.

Johnson rode his black gelding unnoticed down through the jagged rocks and into the town. He steadied the horse and allowed it to walk through the quiet streets on its way to the sheriff's office.

He became aware that the town was unusually empty of people. In all the years that he had visited Cooper's Plain, he had never seen so few people on its boardwalks. Maybe even those who lived here had fled, he thought.

His eyes darted from one building façade to another. He was expecting to see dozens of horses tied to the hitching rails before them, but there were none. The only real noise within the streets of Cooper's Plain was coming from the Lucky Dime saloon, but even that was subdued.

The rancher turned his horse to face the sheriff's office. Dan Johnson dismounted and tied his reins around the cast-iron water-pump next to the full trough. He paused and looked up and down the long quiet street.

It worried him.

The door of the sheriff's office opened and Jake Walker stepped out into the sunshine. Walker was a man who looked the part of a frontier lawman, but in the five years he had held the job, he had never been tested.

'What brings you into town, Dan?'

Johnson stepped up on to the porch and rubbed the dust from his features.

'The westbound stage got held up by half a dozen outlaws, Jake,' he told the sheriff.

Walker's jaw suddenly dropped as the words sank into his brain. The lawman stepped closer to Johnson and stared hard into his eyes. Johnson nodded as if to confirm his statement.

'The stage has been held up?'

'Yep. Two men were killed. A passenger and the shotgun guard. Another passenger had his skull cracked open and a female was assaulted.' Johnson stared at the sheriff's feet as he spoke.

'Where did they go?' the sheriff asked, rubbing his neck and trying to think of what he was meant to do now. He was used to controlling the odd drunk but had no experience of anything more demanding.

'They headed on along the canyon road. They're coming here, Jake,' Johnson muttered with a frown on his face.

'Here? They're coming here?' The sound of panic in the lawman's voice could not be disguised. He bit his lip and tried to think again.

The weary rancher rested a hand against a wooden upright. 'I cut through the peaks to get here and warn you before they show up.'

Walker patted the shoulder of the tall lean rancher. 'I'm grateful that you did, *amigo*. If them outlaws are headed here we gotta get ourselves organized.'

Dan Johnson stepped back down to the dusty street and untied his reins.

'This is your party, Jake. I got business at the bank.'

The sheriff grabbed hold of the rancher's arm and turned him.

'You can't just waltz in here and tell me something like that and then mosey on out. I need men to back me up if there are six killers coming into Cooper's Plain. I need men like you.'

Johnson untied his reins and began to lead the horse away from the sheriff.

'I ain't even got a gun any more, Jake. If the banker don't give me an extension on my loan, I won't have enough to feed my stock.'

Jake Walker stood in the street and watched the tall figure leading the black gelding through the dusty street. He wanted to call out but knew that to do so would sound desperate.

Deputies! I gotta get me some deputies! Walker told himself. He ran across to the saloon.

Sheriff Walker entered through the swing-doors and stared around the saloon. Three men apart from the bartender looked hard at the nervous lawman.

'You look like ya seen a ghost, Jake,' the bartender said as he polished a thimble glass with a white cloth.

'The westbound stage was held up a while back,' Walker said, leaning on the bar counter. 'The outlaws are headed here. I need some deputies.'

The faces of the three saloon customers were blank. None of them liked the brash sheriff and it showed as they all turned their backs on the man.

'Any of you men want to help me out?'

The three men finished their drinks and then strolled out of the Lucky Dime. Walker watched them and felt sweat starting to trickle down his spine beneath his black shirt.

The bartender said nothing as he continued polishing his whiskey glasses.

'What about you, Ed?'

'I reckon that when they arrive I'll be busy serving them drinks, Jake,' the man said honestly. 'With any luck, they'll drink their fill and then head on to the next town.'

Jake Walker pointed at the whiskey bottles lined up in front of the long mirror behind the bartender.

'Give me a whiskey, Ed.'

Before the cork had been pulled from the neck of the black glass bottle, the swing-doors parted. Both men looked up at Hec Martin, the town mayor.

'Did I hear right? Was the stage robbed, Sheriff?' Martin asked loudly.

'Yep, and the bastards are headed here, Hec,' the bartender replied, pouring the whiskey for the lawman.

Martin left as swiftly as he had arrived. The sound of his small feet running down the boardwalk echoed inside the tall wooden building.

'Where's he going in such a hurry?' Ed asked, picking up the silver dollar from the counter.

'To tell Braddock, I reckon,' Walker said. He downed his liquor in one swallow. 'Same again.'

SIX

If arrogance measured a man's size, then Cecil
Braddock the banker would have been a giant. His
belief in his own self-worth had made him hated by
almost everyone who had ever come into contact
with him. But men like Braddock cared nothing for
popularity, they only desired power.

Braddock had made his fortune long before most
of the people in Cooper's Plain had been born. He
had arrived in the town with a trunk full of money
and built his bank. From that day on, he had preyed
on everyone until he controlled over ninety per cent
of everything.

He would lend cash to anyone as long as they had
something he desired for security. It was a simple but
effective ploy that had allowed him to become the
monster he now was.

Like a leech, Braddock sucked the very life-blood
from the weakest in the remote community.

Exactly how Braddock had acquired his original
fortune was one thing he would never reveal. He

claimed to be from back East but his accent had never substantiated it. Rumours had surrounded the portly bald man for decades, but whatever the truth was it would remain a closely guarded secret.

Braddock had watched his latest victim entering the bank in the knowledge that he had the man exactly where he wanted him.

No sooner had the dishevelled rancher walked into the elegant bank foyer than Braddock steered him away from his more prized customers and into his private office.

The entire room shook when the banker closed the door behind him and walked across the marble flooring.

'Thanks for seeing me, Mr Braddock,' Johnson said in a hushed tone. He had never liked this office, it felt too much like a funeral parlour.

'Now what exactly can I do for you, Dan?' It was a cruel question. Braddock knew that there was only one reason for the rancher to be in his bank, and that was money.

The wily businessman had wanted Dan Johnson's five-hundred-acre spread for years and had been unable to get it until the rancher desperately needed to borrow money. From that moment on, Cecil Braddock had him exactly where he wanted him.

Johnson sat down and watched the bald man walking around his desk, then pausing at the window. The rancher did not like talking to the back of any man, but knew that he needed something from the stern figure and would have to hold his temper.

'I'll be straight with you, Mr Braddock,' Johnson began. 'I need a little money for cattle feed.'

Braddock kept his back to the man and sighed heavily.

'But you have not repaid one cent off the last loan, Dan.'

Johnson looked around the office. Its oak panelling was probably worth more than his entire ranch.

'I will when the rain comes,' Johnson said. 'You know I'm good for it.'

Cecil Braddock turned and then sat down in his huge leather chair, snorting loudly whilst tapping his fingertips together.

'You said that last time.'

Johnson looked at the man and clenched his fists. 'I know that but things have been hard this year. Losing my family kinda dented my savings.'

'None of us has had it easy lately, Dan.' Braddock leaned back and looked down the length of his nose at the rancher. 'I've had one rancher after another coming in here pleading poverty.'

Dan Johnson stood and glared down at the man. He could not hide his disgust.

'So you ain't interested in lending me any more money?'

'I'm afraid not.' Braddock smiled. 'In fact I was thinking of getting my lawyer to foreclose.'

'Are you serious?'

'I would imagine that a week from today, I'll own your entire ranch.' Braddock smirked. 'Nothing

45

personal, friend. It's merely business.'

'That ain't the word that I'd have used, Mr Braddock.' Dan Johnson exhaled heavily.

'Remember that you came to me, Dan,' the banker said. 'You signed the loan forms of your own free will.'

Dan Johnson walked slowly to the door and opened it. 'I'm sorry to have troubled you.'

'Any time. Any time.' Braddock grinned.

Suddenly something alerted both men's attention. The frantic voice of Hec Martin echoed around the interior of the bank as he rushed across the foyer toward Braddock's office. The hysterical mayor of Cooper's Plain pushed past the silent Dan Johnson and started to rant about the stagecoach robbery.

The rancher glanced over his shoulder as he reached the sunlight. He paused when he saw the expression on the banker's face alter from smug satisfaction to uncontrollable rage.

It suddenly dawned on Dan Johnson that the strongbox full of golden eagles taken by the six outlaws from the stage must have belonged to Cecil Braddock.

For the first time in six months, the rancher smiled.

SEVEN

Like the leader he was, Rafe Jarrow led his outfit from the front. For years he had dared anyone to challenge him but there had been no takers. Some men were just born leaders and Jarrow was one of that rare élite. As he steadied his mount he smiled.

This town held no fear for the outlaw who had more than ten notches carved into the wooden handles of his matched Colts.

The six riders swooped confidently down the canyon trail road and headed into the long main street. The few people who had been walking down the boardwalks instantly disappeared into the first available doorway when they spied the deadly troop of riders.

The Outfit aimed their horses at the Lucky Dime. It was as if they instinctively knew where the saloon was. The lathered-up mounts were dragged to a halt directly outside the swing-doors and all the men dismounted.

'Now we drink,' Jarrow said.

Their throats were dry and full of trail dust. Each felt that they deserved the liquor that they could almost taste as they looped their reins over the hitching rails in front of the water troughs.

Jarrow stepped up on to the boardwalk first and surveyed Cooper's Plain with a knowing eye. He had seen ghost towns with more life. This was not a town that bred heroes, he could sense it. Folks here wanted to live long fruitless lives, unlike the Outfit.

Joey Franks and Curly Potter joined him under the porch shade and rested their gloved palms on their gun grips. The rest of the hardened outlaws joined them.

'This place is quiet, Rafe,' Franks said uneasily.

'I don't like it,' Curly opined.

'We ain't gonna have no trouble here, boys.'

'How can you be so sure?'

'Can't you smell it?' Jarrow inhaled the dry air.

'Smell what?'

'Fear, boys. This entire town stinks of pure fear,' Jarrow remarked. He turned and entered the saloon. All five of his men followed in single file. The sound of their spurs echoed around the saloon as the six men approached the long bar and the waiting man.

Ed the bartender looked up at the half-dozen men and forced a smile which belied his fear. For he knew what they had done and prayed that they did not decide to use him for target practice.

'Howdy, gents,' the bartender said. 'What'll it be?'

Rafe Jarrow allowed his men to rest their elbows

on the wet counter surface as he strolled to the very end of the bar. He seemed to be checking every inch of the drinking-hole for hidden lawmen. When satisfied that they were the only ones in the Lucky Dime, Jarrow visibly relaxed.

'Six beers and a bottle of whiskey, barkeep,' he said.

Ed quickly placed the first glass under the beer-tap and filled it with the cool liquid. Faster than he had ever served any customers before, the bartender filled all six half-moon glasses and slid them to each of the dust-caked men in turn.

Then he placed a bottle of his best whiskey on the counter, with six thimble glasses. Sweat ran freely down his face as he stood waiting for the men to start shooting the place up.

'What do I owe you?' Jarrow asked.

Ed swallowed hard. He felt like saying that it was on the house, but knew that would alert the half-dozen outlaws to his knowing what they were and what they had done.

'Six bits ought to cover it, stranger.'

Jarrow tossed a golden eagle on to the counter. He saw the bartender pick it up and stare at it.

'A golden eagle!' Ed gasped. 'I ain't ever seen one of these before.'

Jarrow touched the brim of his Stetson. 'Reckon that ought to be enough.'

'I ain't got enough loose change in my register to break this, mister,' Ed said honestly.

'You keep it and your loose change and our glasses

filled.' The narrow eyed outlaw smiled.

Ed grinned. 'Don't you fret none, I ain't gonna let you boys go thirsty.'

Jarrow downed his whiskey and then lifted the beer-glass to his lips. He savoured every drop of the beer as the bartender began the task of refilling all his men's glasses under the brass tap.

'That's mighty fine beer.'

'It washes the dust out of your throat anyway.' Ed nodded as he continued filling the thimble glasses with whiskey.

Jarrow placed his empty beer-glass down and then looked around the large empty saloon.

'Business ain't so good, huh?'

'It's the damn drought. Half the town moved away months ago when the rain failed to come,' the bartender complained.

'You own this saloon?' Red Clyde asked.

The bartender shook his head. 'Nope. Miss Candice owns this place. They say she won it in a poker game.'

Jarrow's eyebrows rose.

'Is Miss Candice young?'

'Kinda young,' came the diplomatic reply.

Rafe Jarrow removed his boot from the brass foot-rail and pushed himself away from the bar. He looked up the staircase where a few doors were visible in the shadows of the landing.

'I knew a woman named Candice once,' Jarrow said aloud as he continued watching the doors above them. 'Is she up there?'

Ed cleared his throat. 'Yeah but she don't like company.'

Jarrow was thoughtful.

'Has she got red hair?'

Ed nodded. 'Red as a sunset. Why?'

The outlaw leader licked his lips. 'Go and ask Miss Candice if she was ever in Dodge City and if she recalls a man named Rafe Jarrow, barkeep.'

Reluctantly the bartender walked from behind the long counter and headed for the stairs. He knew that his employer was not a woman to bother on a hot sunny afternoon, but he had recognized the name of Rafe Jarrow.

Ed climbed up the stairs to the landing and knocked on the first door.

He could feel Jarrow's eyes burning into his back.

EIGHT

There seemed little more the rancher could do once he returned to his ranch, except resign himself to watching what remained of his herd of white-faced cattle dying of starvation. Johnson could butcher them before that happened but there was little meat on their bones. He had thought about giving them to his fellow ranchers but most of them were in the same position as he was, and barely managing to feed the stock they already had.

Without fattening up, the cattle were worthless.

Yet Johnson had worked for half his life building up that herd and was not about to see that destroyed.

Not without a fight anyway.

Cecil Braddock had wanted his small ranch all the time. That information chewed at the rancher's innards like fire. How could he have been so gullible as not to see through the banker's cold-hearted scheming?

He knew that once Braddock put his lawyer on the case, he had no hope of keeping his ranch. His only hope was to repay some of the debt, but how?

Dan Johnson stood inside the shadows of the large livery stable holding on to the reins of his tired horse. It was cool inside this building, unlike the streets of Cooper's Plain. The rancher was tired. More tired than he had ever been.

'You look tuckered out, Dan.'

He watched as Gus Dekker walked toward him. Dekker was not just a man, he was a giant. He hailed from far to the north where the mountain men were bred to be big. Yet for all his size, Dekker had a huge heart and a soft side. He had one flaw in his nature, he trusted people and, people being the way they are, was often taken advantage of.

Johnson leaned against the wooden wall and sighed heavily.

'I guess I am. Don't know why, I ain't done nothing today except ride into town.'

Dekker looked at the man whose clothes hung loose on his tall frame.

'You eaten anything lately?'

'Come to think of it, no I ain't had me a square meal for a long time,' Johnson recalled.

Dekker tied the reins of the horse next to a bale of hay and then led his friend through the shadows to his own room at the back of the livery. He pushed the door open and then pointed at a chair next to a table.

'Sit there,' Dekker ordered. He placed his skillet on top of his stove. 'I'm cooking you some ham and eggs.'

'There ain't no need, Gus. I'm OK,' Johnson said looking around the small makeshift room which held all of the big man's belongings.

Dekker pulled out two thick slices of ham and dropped them into the spitting grease of the pan. 'This ain't gonna be the prettiest meal you've ever had but it'll fix you up.'

'I'm much obliged,' Dan Johnson muttered. He cast an eye on the huge cot pushed up against a wall. He wondered how on earth it managed to take the weight of his friend.

'A man can't even think straight if he's hungry, Dan,' Dekker said, cracking two eggs and dropping them into the hot fat next to the frying bacon.

It took less that fifteen minutes for the simple meal to be cooked and eaten. Johnson finished the sweet coffee and trailed the huge man back into the heart of the livery stable. He watched silently as Dekker fired up his forge and began hammering a piece of metal until it became a horseshoe. Gus Dekker's muscular arms glistened until the job was finished and tossed on to the pile of others.

'Why did you come see old Gus, Dan?' Dekker asked. He lifted a ladle from his water-bucket and drank the refreshing liquid.

Johnson felt uneasy. He was not the kind who asked favours of friends. It did not sit well with him. Yet his mind was filled with the thoughts of his hungry herd and the laughter of Cecil Braddock. He had to swallow his pride.

'I hate to ask, but I'm in a fix, Gus,' Johnson

began. 'My cattle are dying and I need money for feed. I wondered if there was any jobs I could do for you in exchange for a few dollars.'

Gus shook his head.

'I'm sorry, Dan. I'm owed money from half the folks in town but they ain't got it to repay me. If I had some money I'd give it to ya.'

Johnson patted the massive arm. 'I know that. I'm sorry that I had to ask. I didn't want to put you on the spot.'

'Things are sure bad around here.' Dekker sighed as he rested the shovel-sized hand on Johnson's lean shoulder.

'It looks like old man Braddock will take my ranch off me if'n I don't repay my loan. I tried to get him to lend me a little more but he wants my spread.' Dan Johnson ran his fingers through his greying hair and stared out across the bright street at the bank.

'Braddock has managed to pick up three ranches in the last month for nothing.' Dekker sighed. 'I just don't understand folks like him. He was rich when he got here so how come he is so all fired-up getting richer?'

'Some men just can't get enough, I guess.'

'Greed is a darn ugly thing.'

'At least you can be proud that you ain't greedy, Gus.' Dan Johnson looked at the massive man who was rubbing his chin the way men do when they realize that they need a shave.

Dekker was about to respond when he saw Braddock and Mayor Martin rushing from the bank

56

and heading across the street. He tapped the rancher's arm and pointed at the sight. It was one neither of them had ever witnessed before.

'Talk of the devil. I wonder where that old skinflint is heading with the mayor, Dan?' Dekker laughed. 'Anybody would think that his tail's on fire.'

'Maybe it is.' Johnson exhaled heavily.

He stepped beside the stable man and watched the two men rushing down the length of the main street in the direction of the sheriff's office.

'Where they headed, Dan?'

'They were both all fired up with the news that the stage got itself robbed, Gus,' Johnson said. 'I reckon they want Jake to polish his sheriff's star and do something.'

'The stage has been robbed?' Dekker gasped. 'Who by?'

The rancher suddenly noticed the string of horses tied up outside the Lucky Dime saloon. Six lathered-up horses. The same six horses that he had witnessed beside the stagecoach an hour or so earlier.

Johnson pointed a finger at the saloon.

'The owners of that string of horseflesh, Gus,' he said quietly.

NINE

Mayor Hec Martin and Cecil Braddock burst into the sheriff's office but they were both stopped dead in their tracks by the sight that greeted them. It was not what they had either expected or wanted. Seeing Sheriff Jake Walker slumped over his desk with his hand still clutching the empty whiskey bottle filled both men with total shock and anger.

Knowing that the stagecoach had been robbed was bad enough but to also see their paid puppet, Walker, helplessly drunk just added to their confusion. The richest two men in Cooper's Plain moved across the office to the desk.

'Wake up, Jake!' Braddock shouted at the snoring lawman. 'Can you hear me?'

Martin took hold of the dark hair and lifted Walker's head off the ink-blotter. Walker continued snoring loudly.

'He's drunk!' Martin gasped, releasing his grip on the greased hair. The sheriff's head bumped loudly on top of the desk. 'But Jake don't hardly drink at all. I don't get it.'

'He's chosen a grand time to become a lush, Hec,' Braddock fumed. He paced up and down the office trying to think of how he could get his shipment of golden eagles back from the stagecoach robbers. His first plan had been to send Walker out after it with a posse, but that had evaporated as soon as he had spotted the drunken lawman.

'But we need this dumb ox, Cecil.' Martin lifted the coffee-pot up off the stove and raised its lid. It was empty. He banged it back down on top of the stove.

'We have to get that gold back, Hec!' Braddock clenched his fist and ran his knuckles over the scalp of the sheriff. 'Wake up, you useless half-wit.'

'We have to get that money back. Fast!'

'Don't you think I know that?'

'I don't want to end up in prison at my age.'

'We have to remain calm. We have to think this through.'

Martin moved to the side of the larger man and pulled out a cigar from the silk pocket of his tailored coat. He bit off its end and spat it out on to the floor.

'Try and think of something, Cecil.'

Braddock glanced at the mayor.

'I'm trying. But all I know for sure is that if the authorities were to find out about some of our business practices, we'll both be in big trouble. I just don't understand how those damn robbers managed to pick the one stagecoach in a month that we were using to transport the gold.'

'Inside information.' Martin brooded.

'Exactly. We were sold down the river.'

'I thought you said that you had two Pinkerton men on the stage guarding that gold?' Martin struck a match and lifted the flame to the end of his cigar. He puffed and stared at his associate through the smoke.

'I did. And a fat lot of good the idiots were by the sound of it.' Braddock rubbed his sweating palms together and stared out at the Lucky Dime saloon on the corner of the main street. He stepped closer to the open doorway and squinted.

'What's wrong, Cecil?' Martin asked as he saw the expression on Braddock's face alter.

The banker pointed. 'Look over there, Hec. There's six horses tied up outside the saloon.'

The mayor pulled the long cigar from his mouth and screwed up his eyes.

'You're right. But so what? We're in really big trouble if we don't get that gold back and all you can talk about is a bunch of horses. Concentrate, man!'

Braddock grabbed the collar of the mayor and shook the man until he was giddy.

'Who do we know in or around town who has six riders, Hec?' Martin thought for a few seconds.

'Why?'

'There ain't a ranch around here with six riders so those horses don't belong to any of the spreads. Right?' The banker watched the mayor nod in agreement. 'And those horses don't belong to anyone in Cooper's Plain. Right?'

'Right!' Martin was puzzled but agreed.

'So who do you think might own six horses?'

Hec Martin shrugged and sucked on his cigar. 'I don't know. What the hell are you trying to say?'

'The stagecoach robbers.' Braddock leaned down and whispered into the ear of the man he had personally paid hard cash to get elected. A man who was none too bright but always did exactly as he was told.

'Damn! You could be right, Cecil,' the mayor said.

'If I am right, our money is in those saddle-bags.' Braddock stared hard at the swollen bags tied to the saddle cantles.

Martin flicked the ash off his cigar and looked back at the sheriff.

'Which means we gotta sober Jake up real fast.'

Braddock looked at the sheriff.

'I don't think that's possible, Hec. Jake won't wake up this side of Easter. Even if he did I don't think the yellow bastard would face up to those robbers. They're killers and he's just a dude who looks good wearing a star. Why else would he drink himself senseless?'

'But who else could go up against them varmints, Cecil?'

The banker ran a hand over his bald scalp. He had an idea but wondered if it was possible.

'How many able-bodied men are there in town, Hec?'

'A couple of dozen, I guess.'

'Find them and tell them to meet me at the bank.'

Braddock walked out on to the boardwalk with the mayor on his heels.

'But they won't tackle them *hombres*, Cecil.' Martin closed the door behind him. 'Not once we tell them who they are.'

'Tell every able man that I'll pay them fifty dollars a head if they make a citizen's arrest.' Braddock smiled as the two men walked back in the direction of the bank. 'But don't tell them anything about those six riders being stagecoach robbers or killers.'

Mayor Martin sucked on the cigar and chuckled.

'Yeah. Why break a lifetime's habit and suddenly be honest with folks?'

Braddock patted Martin's back. 'You're starting to think like a politician, Hec. It's about time.'

TEN

Candice LeBeau was a name, like the lady herself, that nobody seemed capable of forgetting. She professed to be the only daughter of a rich Louisiana plantation owner but the reality was far less colourful. Mary Reilly had been forced to fend for herself from the start. The daughter of a fallen angel, she had used her wits to claw her way out of the cesspit existence that fate had given her. For two decades the beautiful female had roamed the West using every gift that she possessed to survive. Learning to play poker at the age of five, she had used her beauty and charm to disarm many a better hand. Yet since winning the Lucky Dime she had become almost a recluse and seldom ventured outside her rooms above the saloon.

She had long since lost any desire to act the glamorous hostess and preferred to remain unseen by anyone except her staff. Rumours abounded about why such a natural beauty would choose to hide away and not bathe in the adoration of the men she had grown expert at teasing. Was she ill or had the famed looks finally bowed to the passing of time?

Whatever the reason for her self-imposed exile from the admiring glances of those who loved her, it had lasted now for nearly twelve months, yet after having spoken to Ed the bartender her curiosity had been awakened.

Ed walked slowly down the stairs and back to his bar. All six men watched him but none with the same interest as the deadly Rafe Jarrow.

'Well?' Jarrow asked loudly.

The bartender nodded as their eyes met.

'Miss Candice says she did spend some time in Dodge and she does recall a certain Rafe Jarrow.'

'And?'

'And she invites you up to her room for a drink and polite conversation.' Ed grinned as he saw the hardened outlaw suddenly seem like a young boy on his first date.

Jarrow wished he had time to get the trail dust off him.

'She wants me to go right up?'

'Yep. Miss Candice ain't a lady who likes to be kept waiting, Mr Jarrow.' Ed watched and continued filling the glasses of the other men whilst Rafe Jarrow made his way gingerly to the foot of the stairs.

Curly Potter stared at the wall clock above the bar mirror.

'That stagecoach guard ought to have freed himself by now, boys. Once that coach turns up, things might get ugly.'

Franks nodded and watched Jarrow walking to the

staircase. 'I sure hope Rafe's reunion don't take long. We gotta ride soon if we're gonna get to Smith's Spring before sundown.'

'You got any grub in this place, barkeep?' Talpin asked as he nursed his beer.

'There's a tray of ham sandwiches out in the back room.' Ed replied.

'That'll do.' The outlaw nodded. They watched as Ed slipped into the next room.

'We've bin here too long already!' Red Clyde announced. He watched the door up on the landing curiously as their leader edged nervously towards the bottom step.

'Easy, Red,' Neddy Holmes said quietly, rubbing his hands together as thoughts of females filtered into his immature brain for the umpteenth time that day. 'Rafe wouldn't put us at risk.'

Ed the bartender returned and placed the tray of whopping sandwiches down on the bar. Hands grabbed at the food until only one remained amid the crumbs.

'Is there a brothel in town, barkeep?' Neddy asked the tall bartender.

There was a hesitation in Jarrow's steps which came from a worry deep inside him as he ascended the staircase. Would Candice still look the same as she had done back at Dodge? What if she had grown stout like so many females do once they turn a certain age? But then, how much had he himself altered in all that time? Had the years been kind to him? He thought not.

Jarrow removed his hat and rapped his knuckles across the door three times. The bartender had said that her hair was still as red as a sunset. The outlaw recalled all the times he had touched those flowing red locks. They had been like perfumed silk. Would they still be?

'Come on in, Rafe,' her voice called out from the interior of the room. She sounded exactly as she had done all those years ago, he thought. Jarrow nervously turned the doorknob and pushed it open.

She was sitting in the darkened room on a high-back leather chair. She was wrapped in a red-silk dressing-gown sipping a tall glass of mint tea.

Jarrow could not make her face out clearly. Her long mane of scarlet hair hung draped over the side of her face that was closest to him.

'Candice? Is it really you after all these years?' Jarrow closed the door and hesitantly moved nearer to the one woman who had actually meant something to him.

Miss Candice did not look up at her guest but continued to sip at the glass in her hands.

'It's me OK, Rafe. So many years have been wasted since we last met.'

Her voice was as youthful as ever. It sounded like melted butter to the outlaw as he drew closer to her.

'Why is the room so dark, Candice?'

'I prefer it that way, Rafe. The shadows allow our memories of one another not to be thrust into reality.'

Jarrow sat down on a chair opposite her. He stared

at her long hair and began to wonder why she would not face him. Why she spoke at the wall and not directly at him. A cold shiver traced his backbone.

'You said that you would come back,' Miss Candice said. 'I waited in Dodge for more than a year.'

'I meant to return but . . .'

'Was I just another notch on your gun grip, Rafe?'

'No! You were the only one.' Jarrow felt anxious.

'Have a glass of mint tea.' Her long slender arm gestured at the tray. 'Before you leave me again.'

Rafe Jarrow knew she was right. His time in Cooper's Plain was fast running out and he should have already led his men away from this place to the safety of Smith's Spring. Yet he did not want to leave her again. Not like this.

'It's a long time since I've had a glass of mint tea, Candice.' He lifted the large glass jug and poured the fragrant drink into the tall tumbler.

ELEVEN

Hec Martin had used every ounce of his cunning to wheedle able-bodied men capable of handling a Winchester out from their hiding-places. Then he plied them with as much liquor as was necessary to make them brave. He had managed to rustle up fourteen men altogether.

He triumphantly led them into the foyer of the bank and presented them to Braddock. They were the dregs of an empty barrel by anyone's standards and the banker knew it, but he needed men who would risk their lives cheaply. The thought of making fifty dollars was something none of them could afford to reject out of hand.

The bald banker moved in front of the gathered assembly and tried to look impressed. He began to spin a web of lies that he knew would confuse their drunken brains.

Half-way through his speech, Braddock noticed two figures standing silently behind his naive volunteers. Dan Johnson and Gus Dekker had followed the drunken crowd into the bank.

Braddock cleared his throat and tried to ignore the pair.

'I repeat, I will give fifty dollars to each of the men who go down to the Lucky Dime saloon and return with the six horses that are tied up outside.'

One of the men standing closest to the banker raised a hand.

'Ain't that stealing?'

Braddock roared with laughter. 'Of course not. How can you possibly be stealing when you are working on the side of the law, my friend?'

Hec Martin produced a box full of deputy stars.

'Take one of these each, men.'

Coyly the men accepted the stars and pinned them to their shirts. With a few legal words from the mayor they were sworn in as deputies and then herded past Johnson and Dekker out into the sunshine.

Each of the men accepted the loaded Winchester rifles that had been borrowed from Jake Walker's office. They were then pointed in the direction of the saloon.

'Go get those horses, boys!' Braddock boomed.

The men stood exactly where they were. Slowly, one by one the men turned and faced the banker. One of them stepped forward to the sweating Braddock.

'What if the owners of them nags don't cotton to their horses being borrowed, Mr Braddock?'

The bald man's eyes flashed angrily.

'Then just take the saddle-bags.'

The fourteen men started to wonder what this was all about. Why there was so much urgency. Why would Braddock and Martin not do this themselves, if it were so straightforward. Even for the price of fifty dollars a head, this was beginning to sound a little dangerous.

'The saddle-bags?' one of the men repeated.

'First you said you wanted the horses and now you just want the saddle-bags?' another man added.

'What the hell are you two up to?' a third man asked.

Cecil Braddock waved his arms in the air.

'You misunderstand, my friends. The men who are in the saloon are in possession of stolen property. The mayor and myself are just trying to retrieve it.'

The faces of the gathered men each had the same expression etched upon them.

'So the men in the saloon are thieves?'

Braddock looked at Johnson and Dekker who were standing silently smiling behind the armed deputies. He walked up to them and swallowed hard.

'You get those saddle-bags and I'll pay you a hundred dollars apiece,' the banker whispered.

'You want us to go up against that bunch of gunfighters?' Dan Johnson raised a surprised eyebrow. 'I'm broke, not loco.'

'Five hundred dollars each!' Cecil Braddock said under his breath. 'What do you say?'

'Thanks but I kinda like being alive,' Dekker said.

'Did you hear me? Five hundred dollars! Each!' the banker repeated desperately.

Both Dekker and Johnson looked at one another. They needed the money but knew that there was little chance of collecting their remuneration even if they accepted. Whoever those six outlaws were in the saloon, it was doubtful that they would let anyone get close to their horses.

The two men looked at one another and then turned and started back in the direction of the livery stable.

Braddock grabbed Johnson's arm and turned him round.

'I'll write off all your loans and pay you a thousand dollars in golden eagles each. All you have to do is get those saddle-bags and bring them back to me.'

Dekker and Johnson looked at one another.

Neddy Holmes was growing bored with just drinking. The young outlaw wanted a woman. He had never managed actually to satisfy a woman or even come close to losing his virginity, but he seemed determined to keep trying and create the illusion that he was a real man.

The Lucky Dime was quiet, unlike most frontier saloons.

'This place got any whores, barkeep?' Neddy asked Ed as he placed yet another frothy beer on top of the bar counter.

'Sorry, son,' the bartender replied, shrugging. 'I wish it had but they all left for richer pickings.'

'Then who is this Miss Candice who Rafe has gone visiting?'

The bartender looked angry.

'Miss Candice is the owner of this saloon. She ain't no whore.'

'Then how come Rafe is up in her room?' Neddy kept running his thumb over the hammer of his holstered Colt. He was jealous and it showed.

'They're old friends.'

'Leave the barkeep alone, Neddy,' Joey Franks snarled at the young man. 'What Rafe does ain't none of our business. You remember that and you'll live longer.'

Neddy Holmes stepped away from the bar and rested the palm of his hand on his gun grip.

'I'm thinking that you want me to put a bullet in your big fat mouth, Joey.'

Franks downed his whiskey and glanced at the dangerous young outlaw. He had no fear of this or any of the other members of Jarrow's outfit.

'You draw on me and I'll kill you where ya stand.'

Neddy's eyes twitched. His eyes darted across the faces of four outlaws. They were all staring at him coldly.

'You don't think I'm scared of you boys, do ya?'

'The next town will have plenty of willing females in it, Neddy.' Red Clyde muttered. 'Save them wild oats for a couple of days.'

Neddy growled and walked away from the other men. He stopped and looked out of the long window that faced the main street of Cooper's Plain. As his frustration eased he began to notice a small crowd down at the other end of the long quiet thoroughfare.

'Is there some sort of town meeting going on this afternoon, barkeep?' Neddy called across the saloon.

Ed looked puzzled.

'Not that I'm aware of, son. Why?'

'There must be a dozen or more men down the other end of the street.' Neddy scratched his right sideburn.

'The bank is down there. Maybe folks have heard that you boys are in town and are withdrawing their savings in case you decide to rob it.' Ed chuckled until he realized that all five of the outlaws were staring coldly at him. 'What's wrong?'

'What do you know about us, barkeep?' Curly Potter asked.

Ed cleared his throat and continued serving drinks.

'I don't know nothing.'

Lon Talpin drew his pistol and cocked its hammer and aimed it straight at the sweating man.

'If you don't tell us what you know, I'll blow your head off your shoulders.'

The bartender's mind raced.

'I've heard of the famous Rafe Jarrow. He's a living legend and if you boys are riding with him, I reckon you must all be famous outlaws as well.'

Talpin smiled, eased the hammer of his Colt back down and then holstered the .45.

'We are famous. We're known as the Jarrow gang or the Outfit.'

Ed nodded frantically.

'I heard of you. You boys are the best.'

76

Neddy shook his head as he looked out of the window.

'I don't like the looks of them men, boys.'

Joey Franks marched across the room and looked to where Neddy was pointing. His expression changed.

'Neddy might be right. There are too many of them. Something's up. Get Rafe, Red.'

Clyde bounded up the staircase and banged on the door that they had all watched their leader entering five minutes earlier.

'Rafe! Rafe!'

The door opened and Jarrow stood looking at the young outlaw.

'What's eatin' at you? Why all the ruckus?'

'Looks like there's trouble brewing up the road,' Red Clyde gasped. 'You better come and take a look, Rafe. Me and the boys don't know what to do.'

'Has the stage arrived yet?' Jarrow stared hard at the man but his thoughts were with the female in the room behind him.

'Nope. The stage ain't made it to town yet. Why?'

'Then them varmints don't know who or what we are, do they?' Jarrow explained. 'You boys are just imagining things. Take it easy.'

'But. . . .'

Rafe Jarrow looked over his shoulder into the dark room and then returned his attention to the outlaw.

'I've got some unfinished business here, Red. I ain't your wet-nurse. Just stay calm and alert.'

Jarrow slammed the door in the face of the outlaw.

77

Nervously, Clyde walked down to the other outlaws.

'Well?' Neddy Holmes shouted across the saloon at Red Clyde.

Clyde shrugged.

'Just keep watching that crowd.'

TWELVE

Her voice was soft and yet every single word she uttered made the hardened outlaw feel racked with guilt. He had promised to return to Dodge City and take her with him to a new life. Jarrow stared at the glass in his hands and remembered how empty that promise had been nearly ten years earlier.

'I think that you've left it a little late to return, Rafe,' Candice said bluntly.

There were no excuses for his not returning to her. He knew that. For years Jarrow had blocked all memory of the red-haired beauty from his mind, choosing to find comfort in the whiskey he had grown used to.

'I tried to write but the James brothers didn't like any of the gang sending letters, in case it gave away our hiding-places.' Jarrow did not believe the words he was uttering but knew that the truth was far more cruel. 'Then I was told that you had left Dodge and left no forwarding address.'

'The West is a big place and I am just a small

female.' Her voice faltered for a brief moment.

Jarrow stared at her hair. Even in the dim light of the room its radiance was undiminished. He sighed heavily. Candice LeBeau had been correct. In truth, she had been just another conquest, as she had said ten minutes earlier when he had first entered her room. Or at least that was how it had seemed at first to the ruthless outlaw. Before he had had time to compare her with all the females he would later encounter.

In his own way, he had loved her.

'I waited and waited. Like the foolish young thing I was back then, Rafe. I just waited.' Her voice seemed slightly louder as she rose to her feet and floated across the room to the window. The drapes were drawn and she toyed with the edge of the colourful material. 'I thought we were going to create a new life for ourselves back East or even in California. Away from the people who knew your name and what you did for a living.'

Jarrow stood up from the chair and faced her. He inhaled deeply. She still wore the same perfume that had entranced him all those years earlier.

'There ain't no excuses worth a damn, Candice. I rode out and could have come back to you but I just decided that it might be best for both of us if I continued riding. I had this damn stupid idea that I'd forget all about you and find another.'

'Did you find others?'

'Nope. I never did.' For the first time he was telling her the truth. Since the last time he had been in her arms, there had been no one else. He had met a hundred women but none had ever rekindled the flame inside him. She had no equal. 'What did you mean, that I've arrived too late, Candice?'

'Your gang seem anxious that you get going.' She glanced across at him and expertly changed the subject. He still could not see her features clearly. 'I think that it must be time for you to leave town, Rafe.'

'They can wait. I'm not ready to leave you just yet,' he drawled. He stepped closer to her. 'In fact I've lost all interest in going anywhere, without you.'

Miss Candice's small delicate hand was raised as if silently begging him to keep his distance. He ignored her mute plea and continued until it pressed into his dusty shirt. She turned her head away again.

'Go now, Rafe. Just go. Please.' There was something in her lovely voice that he had never heard before. It was defeat.

It troubled him more than anything had done before.

This was not a woman who surrendered willingly to anything or have anyone, yet she seemed to have lost faith in everything.

He wondered why.

Surely it could not have anything to do with his leaving her all those years earlier. Or could it?

The question burned into his craw.

Jarrow took her small hand in his and refused to release it from his strong grip. He could feel it shaking and wondered why. Was she afraid of him? If so, why? He lifted it and pressed it to his dry, cracked lips.

'I've never stopped loving you, Candice.'

'The girl you once loved is dead. Go now with your men. They need you and I don't.' Her words were cruel yet did not fool the outlaw. He had known every ounce of this female once and instinctively knew when she was lying.

The outlaw leader listened to her words and refused to believe any of them. There was no bitterness in her voice, only sorrow.

'Who the hell are you trying to kid, Candice?'

She turned and faced him for the first time. Her free hand pulled back the drape and allowed the afternoon light to flood into the room. Then she pulled her hair off her face revealing the black cancerous patch of skin that had destroyed half her once perfect profile.

'Look at me, Rafe. What do you see?'

His eyes narrowed.

'I see the most beautiful woman I've ever had the honour of knowing, Candice.'

She tried to protest but he pulled her into his arms. He inhaled her soft hair. It was still the same.

'I'm dying, Rafe. I've been unable to eat anything solid for weeks and exist only on liquids. How long do you think I've got? Another week or maybe two? How long do you think I can take the constant pain?'

'If only I'd not wasted all those damn years,' Jarrow said through gritted teeth.

'Your gang need you. I'm beyond anyone's ability to help.'

Rafe Jarrow thought about his men down below in the bar and the money in their saddle-bags. He had provided well for them. He had taught them well and knew that they no longer needed him.

Yet to remain here could prove suicidal.

Jarrow held her close but felt that his arms might crush her delicate frame if he were to hug her too tightly. For the first time in his life, the thought of death held no fears for the outlaw leader.

'I'll tell my boys to ride on out. I'm staying with you. I promise you that I'll never leave you again,' he whispered into her perfumed hair.

'They'll kill you!' Her voice shook.

'They'll try!'

THIRTEEN

Ten out of the fourteen newly deputized lawmen left Braddock and Martin at the bank after Dan Johnson and the stable man had declined the banker's offer. Hard liquor had a way of making even the most level-headed of souls embark on journeys that they might never even consider whilst totally sober.

These men knew nothing of fighting but with the loaded weaponry in their hands and the promise of fifty dollars still in their heads, they advanced toward the Lucky Dime saloon.

Braddock had told them. All they had to do was bring the six horses back to him. Should the owners of the horses get angry with them, their deputy stars gave them the power to use deadly force. The law was on their side.

But these ten men needed more than the law on their side, they needed somebody who knew what the hell he was doing. Somebody who could hit what he was aiming at with the loaded Winchester.

None of the ten deputies had any idea of what was

going to happen once they made their play. This was a can of worms which beggared description.

This was suicidal.

Yet they were making their way down to the saloon in what appeared, at first glance, a sensible way. The men had split their meagre force into two groups. One of six and the other of four.

The six men were going for the horses tied to the hitching poles outside the saloon whilst the other quartet had decided that they would go round to the rear of the Lucky Dime and burst in on the Outfit from behind.

To men who had a quart of whiskey in each of their bellies, this seemed a perfect plan.

What could go wrong?

Had any one of them possessed even a granule of imagination in what passed for a brain, they would have known what could go wrong.

Everything!

But Braddock and Martin had not told these men the whole truth when they had dispatched them. They had not revealed the fact that these were a gang of deadly stagecoach robbers. Men who killed just for the sheer pleasure of it.

The six deputies had one building between themselves and the saloon. They watched their four colleagues moving to the rear of the saloon. Suddenly the men stopped in their tracks as the ground rumbled beneath their feet. The stagecoach came thundering down the trail road and turned into the main street of Cooper's Plain. Sagebrush

86

steered the six-horse team with an expertise that only time itself afforded.

Gus Dekker was the first to reach the vehicle and help the passengers into the doctor's office. Johnson watched the weathered old-timer climb down from the high driver's seat.

Dan Johnson curled a finger at Hec Martin and watched the man advance on him. The rancher pulled back the heavy tarp from the rear of the stage-coach and revealed the body of the less fortunate passenger.

Martin gasped in horror when his eyes focused on the body with half its head blown away. The mayor turned and was sick all over the large wheel-rim.

'Who is that?' Martin managed to ask a few moments later.

'Don't know his name,' Sagebrush answered, scratching his beard. 'But that's what them robbers is capable of, sonny. They is a real mean bunch of varmints and no mistake.'

Johnson lifted the dead man out of the luggage tail-gate of the coach and carried him towards Cecil Braddock.

The banker was frozen to the spot as the rancher approached him.

'Keep that away from me, Johnson!'

Johnson dropped the body at the banker's feet.

'Take a good look, Braddock. You've just sent ten men into the jaws of the animals that did this. Reckon there'll be quite a few more by the time that gang are through.'

Braddock turned away and stared at the distant saloon.

'Those men will not have any trouble with those outlaws.'

'You just keep telling yourself that but don't expect anyone else to believe it, Braddock.' Johnson turned and walked back to Sagebrush and Dekker.

Down the other end of the long dry street the deputies cocked the Winchesters and waited in the shadows for their chance to reach the six skittish mounts.

Inside the Lucky Dime the five outlaws had watched the dust rising off the hoofs and wheels of the rocking vehicle as it travelled away from them towards the stage depot near the livery.

'Now we're on borrowed time!' Joey Franks exclaimed, turning to the other men. 'Get Rafe down here. Now!'

Reluctantly, Red Clyde made his way up the staircase again and started knocking on the wooden surface of the door.

'Rafe! The stagecoach has showed up! Joey wants you down there.'

A few seconds later the door was opened. The outlaw leader came out of the room and hurried down into the heart of the Lucky Dime.

Rafe Jarrow rushed to the window and pushed Neddy Holmes aside to look down the long street. The dust was swirling in the dry air, making it impossible to see anything clearly.

'Lon?' Jarrow called across the saloon.

Talpin came across to the window. 'Yep?'

'There's still time. It'll take them half-wits a while to figure out what's going on. You fill the canteens.'

Lon Talpin touched the brim of his Stetson, walked through the swing-doors and pulled all six canteens off the saddles. He started to fill them from the water-pump next to the trough.

'We ain't got no provisions, Rafe,' Franks said.

'There ain't no time to get any now.' Jarrow squared up to his men as he watched Lon Talpin trying to fill their canteens. 'I got some news for you, boys.'

Franks stared at Jarrow.

'What sort of news?'

'You boys will be heading on to Smith's Spring without me.'

Franks moved next to the older man. He had never seen him like this before and it troubled him.

'We ride together or not at all, Rafe.'

Jarrow looked at the men whom he had guided for years. They had never once managed to make a decision without him. He wondered whether they could fend for themselves.

'The money is all in your saddle-bags, not mine. You ride to the next town and I'll catch up when I can.'

'What's wrong, Rafe?' Potter asked.

Jarrow glanced up at the door to Miss Candice's room then back at his men. 'I can't explain right now. There ain't time. Look, you have to get the money away from here.'

Joey Franks could see that there was no chance of talking the older outlaw round. He had made up his mind.

'Come on, boys. Rafe knows what he's doing. Let's cut out of this dust-bowl town.'

Suddenly, the door to the rear room burst open and the four deputies piled into the saloon. Their rifles began to spit lead at the Outfit. Bullets flashed across the length of the Lucky Dime. Wood splintered everywhere.

Jarrow was first to draw his Colts. He began firing back at the deputies. Curly Potter was hit high in the chest and sent flying through the huge window.

'Get going, boys!' Jarrow screamed above the sound of the relentless gunfire.

His men moved out on to the boardwalk as the six other deputies started firing from their hiding-places across the street. Talpin was knocked off his heels by a rifle bullet but somehow managed to get back to his feet. Blood was pouring from the outlaw's chest as he drew one of his Colts.

Rafe Jarrow stood in the doorway and shouted at his gang.

'Mount up and ride!' he ordered.

Bullets tore through the hot air and the leader of the Outfit felt an agonizing pain in his side. He staggered back and fell between the horses as his remaining men tried to mount up. Jarrow pulled the hammers of his guns back and blasted two of the men inside the saloon.

90

Deafening gunshots drowned out the screams of the men and horses being caught in the crossfire.

Somehow Jarrow managed to get back to his feet and fire again. He gritted his teeth and tried to get back to the smoke-filled saloon where he knew the dying female waited for him, but it was no use.

Bullets ripped the boardwalk apart and he knew that the two men inside the building were not going to let him return to Miss Candice. They now had the choking gunsmoke to shield them from the eyes of the lethal marksmen.

Joey Franks had already torn his own Winchester from its scabbard beneath his saddle and was firing angrily at their attackers. He saw one of the deputies fall backwards and then another slump head first into the dust. Bullets from inside the saloon continued to come at him. He fired and knocked one of the men off his feet. Franks watched as the man crashed into the long bar but was amazed when the man continued firing his rifle back at him.

Franks leapt on to his saddle and grabbed hold of the reins to one of the spare horses. He glanced down at his dead friend Curly and cranked the mechanism of his Winchester again. He fired continuously at the deputies, giving cover to Neddy and Red until they too had managed to mount their own horses.

Grabbing at the reins of his mount, Jarrow had hauled himself on to his saddle, when he saw Lon Talpin being torn apart by the lethal lead of the

91

carbines. As the outlaw hit the ground all six canteens fell into the dust.

Suddenly Jarrow felt his horse collapsing beneath him when the deputies' crossfire found the huge target. The outlaw scrambled from the saddle and accepted the reins to Talpin's mount from Franks.

Rafe Jarrow ran the horse for a dozen paces before throwing himself over its saddle.

'Ride!' Jarrow called out to his men as he drove his terrified mount away from the saloon. He spurred the horse and galloped along the trail that led to Smith's Spring. Looking over his shoulder he saw Franks, Clyde and Neddy close behind him. Red Clyde had the reins of Curly Potter's horse in his firm but bloody grip.

The four surviving members of the notorious Outfit galloped along the twisting road. To their right rose tall dry brush whilst to their left shimmered a vast expanse of flat glistening salt that seemed to go on for ever. The riders pushed their horses far beyond the wretched creatures' dwindling strength. They had to put distance between themselves and the long rifles of Cooper's Plain before they could stop to check their wounded.

Jarrow knew that they had left their canteens in the pool of blood on the boardwalk of the Lucky Dime saloon. This was not a land to travel in without water.

With every stride that the mounts made, Rafe Jarrow knew that once again he had broken his promise to Miss Candice.

But with blood pouring from his side, he knew he had more pressing things to sort out first.

Survival, his and his men's, being just one of them.

FOURTEEN

It was carnage. The rancher had never seen anything that came close to this horrific spectacle. Dan Johnson took no pleasure in the sight which greeted his eyes and those of the other men who stood behind his broad shoulders.

This had not been a fight. It had been a bloody battle.

None of the deputies had survived unscathed.

Seven were already dead and the other three as close as it was possible to get without actually shaking hands with the Devil himself. Two of the infamous Outfit lay lifeless in their own blood outside the saloon.

Johnson glanced over his shoulder at the faces of Braddock and Martin. They were shocked at what the six outlaws had been capable of and it showed. Yet neither man felt even the slightest guilt that this was their doing.

Braddock headed to the injured horse with only one thought in his mind. Dan Johnson looked down at the pathetic animal as it kicked out at the very ground that it lay upon. He had never seen so many bullet holes in anything before and it turned his guts.

'Give me your pistol, Martin,' the rancher said, holding his hand out to the town mayor. Hec Martin pulled the .44 from his holster and handed it to the rancher.

Johnson checked the gun, cocked its hammer and aimed at the horse's head. He squeezed the trigger and put the animal out of its misery. The sound of the single shot echoed around the town long after Johnson had given the pistol back to the mayor.

The banker moved to the dead horse and knelt down by the saddle-bags. Braddock opened both of the leather flaps and soon found that there were no golden eagles inside. The money must be in the bags of the other horses.

His anger could not be hidden from any of the gathered witnesses.

'Damn it!' he raged.

The one horse that did not carry any of the stolen gold in its leather satchels had been the only one to be killed by the deputies' carbines.

Hec Martin held a hand to his mouth when he stepped next to the bald man. Even now, only a few moments after the raging gun-battle, the stench of death filled the air.

'I thought you said that the gold was in the saddle-bags, Cecil?'

'It seems that not all the bags had our money in it,

96

Hec,' Braddock snarled. 'I don't know about you but I'm having a real bad day!'

'We need somebody to go after those outlaws,' Martin said.

Braddock put his fingers to his associate's lips; his eyes remained fixed on Johnson.

'Hush up. Let me see what I can do in that department.'

Gus Dekker wandered through the bodies, then came to the rancher.

'This is bad, Dan. Real bad.'

Johnson nodded.

'Yep.'

The elderly stagecoach-driver moved from one body to the next, trying to find one with breath still in its lungs. By the time he too had reached the rancher, he had admitted defeat.

'Them outlaws sure know how to shoot, boys.'

'They know how to kill, Sagebrush. There's a difference. A real big difference.'

'What ya mean, Dan?' Dekker asked.

'We all know how to shoot. We hunt to put food in our bellies but them outlaws just kill.'

The two other men nodded in agreement.

Sagebrush looked at Braddock and Martin. He raised a white eyebrow.

'What are them two critters gabbing about?'

'Money!' Johnson said simply as he stepped on to the boardwalk and gazed down at the blood and broken glass which covered the body of Curly Potts.

'They never look so dangerous when they is dead,

do they.' The stagecoach driver sniffed.

'That's 'coz they ain't dangerous once they're dead,' Dekker said. He strode next to the two men who carefully stepped where there was no blood.

'They lost two men. A third of their gang,' Johnson remarked, looking at the bullet-riddled bodies of the outlaws. 'It's a fair bet that the four who managed to ride away from here are wounded.'

'So?' Dekker asked.

The rancher shrugged.

'The odds ain't so great any more.'

'But you said it yourself, Dan. Them critters are killers and we ain't.' Dekker knew that the rancher had something in mind which he did not like even to think about. 'A wounded animal can be even more dangerous.'

'Depends on how wounded they are, Gus.' Johnson raised an eyebrow. He knew that Braddock was desperate to get that gold back at any cost, for some reason.

'You ain't considering Braddock's offer, are ya?' the stable-man looked hard at the lean rancher.

'Could be.'

Dekker looked across at the banker and the mayor, then leaned close to the brooding Johnson.

'But we agreed that it would be certain death to go after them *hombres*. Look around you, Dan. This gang ain't the kind to take prisoners.'

Johnson sighed.

'Sometimes a man has to weigh up the odds, Gus. We both need money in order to survive and for some reason that bald banker has a hankering to part with some of his fortune. I know that going up against that gang is dangerous, but frankly, I don't care.'

'But you could get yourself killed, Dan.' There was concern in the voice of the livery-stable man.

'I've been dead for quite a while,' Johnson said.

All three paused by the swing-doors of the saloon. The wood was blasted to shreds on both doors. They were barely being supported by their hinges.

'I don't like the smell of death,' Dekker said.

'Me neither,' Sagebrush agreed.

'All I can smell is gunsmoke,' Johnson said, pushing his way into the interior of the saloon.

FIFTEEN

Theirs was a trail that anyone could have followed. A bloody trail that led from the sun-baked streets of Cooper's Plain straight to the stunned riders.

Once the four surviving outlaws had been certain that they were not being followed they reined in and stopped riding. Rafe Jarrow knew that they now must be at least five miles from Cooper's Plain and probably twice that distance away from Smith's Spring. But there was no way of checking any longer, for the crude map that had served them well since leaving the badlands was now covered in blood.

His blood.

Jarrow first spotted the telegraph poles which lined the trail road as soon as he and his three followers had ridden out of the town. The swaying wires above them hummed in the afternoon sun. He knew that news of their bloody battle back at Cooper's Plain must already have reached Smith's Spring and every other town due south.

Jarrow knew that it was probably too late to stop a

posse coming after them from Smith's Spring but he still drew one of his Colts and fired. He watched as his deadly accurate aim split the wires in two.

The horsemen slowly dismounted and tried to take stock of their situation. The three younger outlaws had been so fired up by the unexpected attack on them back in Cooper's Plain that they were not even sure whether they had been wounded themselves.

Rafe Jarrow sat down on a boulder and tried to reload his gun, but his fingers were covered in so much of his own blood that the bullets kept falling into the sand at his feet.

Joey Franks checked his horse and was relieved to find that the animal had escaped unscathed. It was not such good news for Neddy Holmes and Red Clyde though. Both their mounts had caught lead and were bleeding badly. The spare horse was unin-jured and yet seemed to be snorting continuously.

'What's the matter with this stupid nag?' Neddy shouted at the ground.

'It knows its master is dead, son,' Jarrow said, look-ing at his men. 'Some critters are a tad sentimental.'

'Are you serious?' Holmes asked the wounded Jarrow. 'How much blood have you lost to start talk-ing rubbish like that, Rafe?'

Jarrow forced a smile.

'We're in trouble, Neddy. Maybe that horse knows it even if you don't. Unlike you, that gelding has horse sense.'

The youngest member of the Outfit pointed down the trail road defiantly.

'How can we be in trouble? We can't be far from the next town. They don't know us there, do they?'

Jarrow pressed his hand into the still-bleeding wound in his side and blinked hard. He was racked with pain and knew that their troubles were far from over.

'And we can't go there, Neddy.'

Holmes's face went suddenly serious. He moved across the dry dusty road and looked hard at the unwontedly quiet outlaw.

'Why not? It can't be more than ten miles to that town. There we can get food and women.'

Jarrow looked up at him. For years he had hoped that Neddy would grow up, but knew that there were some people who could never manage that simple feat. Jarrow would have kicked the youngster if he had been slightly closer.

'Them varmints back there in Cooper's Plain have more than likely wired Smith's Spring, tipping them off that we're heading there, you dumb ass. I don't wanna end up riding into the barrels of another bunch of lawmen.'

Neddy Holmes kicked at the ground.

'But you shot the wires down, Rafe.'

'They had plenty of time to send a message before I even noticed them wires.' Jarrow looked at his blood-soaked hand and rubbed it down his pants leg.

Joey Franks suddenly realized that the one man he had always considered invulnerable was in fact badly wounded. He rushed to the older outlaw and knelt.

'Let me see,' Franks said, pulling the man's jacket

aside. He stared at the torn shirt, then carefully peeled the blood-soaked material from the ugly wound. His eyes narrowed.

'Well?' Jarrow asked the outlaw.

'The bullet went straight through but took six inches of flesh with it. You need to see a doctor, Rafe. You're losing a lotta blood.' Franks looked around. 'Damn, we need water. This has gotta be cleaned up and sewn together.'

'Quit worrying.' Jarrow stood. 'I'm in better condition than Curly and Lon.'

The outlaw leader looked at their horses. He cleared his throat and pointed at the most badly injured horse. It was in a sorrowful state. Jarrow wondered how it was still managing to stand under the weight of its saddle.

'Take the saddle off that horse and put its saddle-bags on to Joey's mount,' he ordered Clyde.

Red Clyde nodded. He lifted the stirrup and hooked it on to the saddle horn. He unbuckled the cinch strap and dragged the saddle off the horse.

'We still only have three horses worth a damn, Rafe,' Neddy said, looking at the other wounded animal.

'It don't matter none.' Jarrow looked out across the salt flats. 'We ain't going to ride for quite a while.'

'What you mean?' Franks asked, tying the heavy gold-filled saddle-bags to his cantle.

'Because we're walking our horses across that salt desert, Joey,' Rafe Jarrow told him.

The three younger men looked at Jarrow in disbelief. Only Neddy Holmes was brave or stupid enough to say anything to their injured leader.

'But that's plain loco!'

Rafe Jarrow stepped closer to the loud-mouthed outlaw. He smiled and then suddenly mustered all his strength to smash his right fist into the youngest outlaw's jaw. Holmes was lifted off his feet and went head over heels across the dust.

'Damn,' Neddy blurted groggily, 'that was sudden.'

'Maybe now you'll be smart enough to keep that mouth of yours shut,' spat Franks. 'We have to hide out in the brush until sundown and then we'll try to make our way across those salt flats. I reckon that we can get back to Cooper's Plain before dawn.'

'What the hell do you wanna go back there for, Rafe?' Red Clyde asked. He tossed the blood-covered saddle into the heavy brush.

'Water and fresh mounts,' Rafe Jarrow said through gritted teeth.

The other three men knew that there was a further reason for their leader wanting to get back to the place from which they had only just managed to escape with their lives. And it had nothing to do with either horses or water. Yet none of them said anything.

SIXTEEN

It had been the most brutal episode in the history of the small town, the like of which nobody wished to see repeated. The bodies were stacked in the undertaker's office waiting for the elderly proprietor to make enough additional coffins. The tally had risen to eight dead by the time Dan Johnson walked into the bank.

The rancher faced Braddock and Martin alone. He followed the two jittery men silently into the large office and sat down whilst the banker took his own seat and the mayor stood next to the magnificent bureau.

'I'm listening,' Johnson said quietly.

'Five hundred dollars and I'll clear your debt,' the wily banker said from behind the large desk.

Johnson watched the sweat trickling down the side of the banker's face and shook his head. Braddock might have been a skilled businessman but he was no poker player.

'An hour ago the price was a thousand dollars for

both Gus and me, and our debts cleared.'

Braddock glanced at Martin who was standing silently in the corner of the office, then returned his attention to the rancher.

'But you declined that offer. It was my best bid.'

'I want two thousand dollars for both me and Gus, plus our loan agreements torn up, Braddock.' Johnson accepted a long cool glass of water from the mayor and nodded.

'Two thousand dollars? Are you mad?' Braddock boomed. 'Why should I agree to those terms?'

'Because you want the gold from those saddle-bags back and there just ain't nobody else left that's dumb enough to try and get it, Braddock.' Johnson downed the water and placed the empty glass on top of the large desk.

'OK. OK. I agree. I'll settle with you when you bring back the gold.' The banker turned his chair and stared at the window. The sun was setting now.

Johnson rubbed his unshaven chin thoughtfully.

'Turn around and look at me, you ignorant swine.'

Braddock's head turned slowly in disbelief. No one had spoken to him like that in fifty years. His expression was wide-eyed and open-mouthed.

'What did you say?'

'I told you to look at me.' Johnson stood and rested one hand on the ink-blotter, waving a finger of the other hand under the fat nose of the bald man. 'I'm calling the shots here, Braddock. I want a strong horse with a good saddle. Mayor Martin's stallion will do fine. I want the loan papers in my hand and I want exactly four thousand dollars in cash. Now stop puffing your cheeks out like some kinda monkey and do as I say. Otherwise I'm riding back to my ranch and them outlaws will just keep on heading south with your money from the strongbox.'

Hec Martin stepped closer to the banker.

'Dan's right, Cecil. Do as he says or those outlaws will get clean away with all the golden eagles.'

The banker pushed his index finger into his stiff collar and pulled it away from his soft thick neck. He knew Johnson was right. They had no choice if they wanted even a slim chance of getting their gold shipment back. Braddock grabbed a cigar from the silver humidor and placed it between his teeth.

'Get the head clerk in here, Hec,' he mumbled. 'Looks like I'm doing business with this dust-caked bastard.'

Martin walked hurriedly from the office.

Dan Johnson continued to stare at the bald man. He had never managed to master the art of actually making money. Until now.

'What makes you think that you are up to this job, Dan?'

Johnson stared at the man and helped himself to one of the cigars. He inhaled its aroma.

'I'll catch them and get your money back, Braddock. You see, I've got an advantage on them outlaws.'

'Advantage?'

'Yep. You see I've lost everything I ever held dear in my life. I don't care how good they might be with

109

their guns because I ain't afraid of dying.'

'You'd better not get yourself killed before you bring that money back to me,' Braddock said coldy.

The cashier entered the office.

'Yes, Mr Braddock?'

'Bring four thousand dollars from the safe and all loan documents concerning Dan Johnson and Gus Dekker,' the banker ordered.

Johnson stared hard and confidently at the man.

'I'll need a good rifle and a Colt with a holster.'

'And ammunition?'

The rancher pushed his tongue into his cheek.

'Yep. Ammunition as well.'

The banker struck a match and offered the flame to Johnson before lighting his own cigar.

'Y'know something? I got me a feeling that them outlaws might be in for a real bad time, Dan.'

Johnson exhaled a line of smoke.

'It's strange what a man will do to feed his stock.'

SEVENTEEN

Dekker finished saddling the mayor's prize stallion and then glanced under the brim of his battered hat at the rancher, who had been sitting in the corner of the livery stable watching the sun getting lower and lower in the cloudless sky. For twenty minutes the undernourished man had hardly spoken a word.

Dan Johnson slipped the Winchester and scabbard beneath the cinch strap, then hung three full canteens on the saddle horn. With every chore Dekker kept looking at the silent rancher, who now sported a new shooting-rig strapped around his narrow hips.

'OK. I give up. What's eatin' you, Gus?' Dan Johnson asked.

The huge man moved quickly across his stable until he was next to the thoughtful rancher. He looked down on the seated figure.

'What was the terms you and old Braddock agreed, Dan?'

Johnson could see the excitement in the man's

eyes. It was like looking at an overgrown child.

'They were good.' He smiled.

'How good?'

The rancher reached inside his shirt and pulled out a large, brown, bulging envelope. He lifted up the paper flap and reached inside whilst the livery owner looked on. Johnson pulled out the legal papers that they had both signed with the banker when times had become even tougher than normal. He handed Dekker his papers and then stared at his own. The words PAID IN FULL were written across both of them and signed by Braddock.

'You got that old skinflint to give you these?' Dekker grinned broadly.

'Yep.' Johnson smiled. 'Now we don't owe that sidewinder a red cent, Gus.'

Dekker kissed the document and then watched his friend pulling out a large wad of bank-notes. Each one was a fifty-dollar bill.

'How much money did he give ya, boy?'

'I managed to get him to part with four thousand dollars.' Dan Johnson handed the money and his own loan document to Dekker. He rose to his feet. 'Half each.'

Gus Dekker was confused.

'What ya giving this to me for?' he asked.

Dan Johnson tied the leather lace which hung from the brand-new holster around his right thigh and checked the Colt .45 carefully.

'Half that money is yours, Gus. Just hold on to my share for me until I return.'

'But I thought we was going together?' Dekker said.

'No, I'm riding alone.'

'But why?'

'There ain't no horse alive that could carry you and manage to walk at the same time.' The rancher sighed. 'Besides, I need you here to buy feed for my cattle and take it out on a buckboard to the ranch.'

'How long do you figure catching them outlaws will take anyway, Dan?' the livery owner asked anxiously.

'Might be a few hours or it could take days. Maybe even longer.' Johnson shrugged.

Dekker looked concerned.

'You are coming back ain't you?'

Johnson stared at the sun. It was now just above the roof-tops and sinking fast. The sky was red like the blood they had both seen spilled that afternoon.

'I'm planning to give that my best effort but sometimes things can go wrong. Just look after my ranch and make sure them steers get grub.'

'I'll start loading a buckboard with feed as soon as you ride out, Dan,' promised Dekker. 'I'll take it up to your ranch at first light tomorrow.'

Johnson nodded.

Dekker watched silently. The rancher held the saddle horn in his grip, stepped into the stirrup and mounted the powerful horse.

'Reckon this stallion will catch up with them outlaws, Gus?'

Dekker sighed. 'Reckon so, Dan. He's a beauty.'

The rancher tapped his boots into the horse's sides. It cantered down the long street, away from the livery stable. As Dan Johnson rode beneath the balcony of the Lucky Dime saloon he thought that he saw the outline of a female in the window.

As he hit the trail road, Johnson felt the strong stallion finding its own pace. In less than a hundred yards the horse was in full gallop.

Johnson had no idea what lay ahead, but whatever it was, he knew it could not be as painful as the memories that haunted his every waking moment.

EIGHTEEN

The sound of thundering hoofs filled the ears of the four remaining outlaws just after they had led their horses out on to the white salt-flats. Somebody was heading from the small town at a tremendous rate.

After sunset, they had walked a hundred yards away from the very edge of the crystallized desert and could see the lights of Cooper's Plain in the distance. The men wondered if the rider was seeking them.

It seemed insane for anyone to do so but they had faced many maniacs before.

They had spent over an hour hiding in the brush whilst waiting for darkness to come. In all of that time no one had passed their hiding-place. Now they could hear somebody riding as if pursued by Satan himself along the dusty road.

Darkness had come swiftly, yet the large moon

overhead cast an unwelcome and eerie light over everything. The four men knew that they were an easy target for anyone who happened to look out at the desolate salt-flats, but the strange light played tricks on their tired eyes. Even now the shimmering heat haze rose from the salty ground, blurring their vision. Nothing was as it appeared and the outlaws knew it.

The sound of the galloping horse grew even louder. The four members of the infamous Outfit stopped in their tracks and stared at the trail road. The noise echoed all around the vast salt-flats, making the thirsty men feel that they were surrounded.

It was not an idea that any of them relished.

'How many are there, Rafe?' Neddy Holmes asked the weakened outlaw, who was still losing blood from his gaping wound.

They could hear the rider galloping along the hard-baked ground but found it difficult to see him. The trail road was set between an avenue of withered trees and brush. But if they could see him, then he could see them, Jarrow thought.

Rafe Jarrow rested a hand on the saddle horn of his mount and narrowed his eyes. He was first to spot the rising dust in the moonlight.

'I'd bet on just one, Neddy.'

He pointed a finger and his three followers stared in the direction that he indicated.

'I see him, Rafe,' Joey Franks said, pulling one of his pistols from its holster and cocking the hammer.

116

Jarrow looked around them and then cursed the brilliant moon in the cloudless sky above them. The blue light was almost as bright as a noonday sun.

'Come on. We ain't got time to waste if we want to reach that town before sun-up.' There was an urgency in the outlaw leader's voice. He could feel his life-force leaving him with each beat of his racing heart.

Franks touched his leader's sleeve, causing the injured man to pause. Their eyes met.

'Let me and the boys head back to the road, Rafe. We'll pick the bastard off his horse as soon as he comes into range.'

It sounded good to Jarrow. He steadied himself and tried vainly to straighten up. But the pain held him in check.

'We could use a good horse to replace the injured one, I guess.'

Franks made as though to move, then he felt the shaking hand tap his shoulder. He turned and looked back at Jarrow.

'What?'

'Leave Neddy with me to lead the horses. You and Red can deal with whoever that is kicking up all that dust, Joey.' Jarrow's words were confident and made the young outlaw feel ten feet tall.

'OK.' Franks smiled and gave the reins to Neddy Holmes. He took Red Clyde with him across the soft, salty ground.

The two men hurriedly followed their own tracks

over the salt-crystals back to the brush and trees that fringed the long twisting road which led from Cooper's Plain to Smith's Spring.

Both outlaws crawled into the brush and aimed their guns at the quickly approaching rider.

'Don't hit the horse. Rafe wants the horse, Red,' Franks said as he tried to get a bead on the horseman who bounced up and down in his saddle. It was an almost impossible shot from where they were lying. The powerful stallion seemed to be filling their entire line of fire.

'I gotta get up to make this shot,' Red said, clambering to his feet.

Joey Franks knew his friend was right.

They simply did not have a big enough target to aim at. With every passing heartbeat the rider drew closer and closer. Franks jumped to his feet and held his gun at arm's length, trying to focus down the gunbarrel sight.

'Damn!' Franks growled. He was angry.

In the eerie light of the moon and with the amount of dust being kicked up from the hoofs of the massive stallion, he knew that even he could not be certain of hitting just the rider.

'What'll we do, Joey,' Clyde asked desperately, knowing that they were fast running out of time. 'I can't even see the rider no more. Should I bring down the horse? Well?'

Franks had to make a decision now.

They had less than twenty seconds before the horseman would reach the brush where they were concealing themselves.

There was no time to think. Jarrow wanted the horse but they both knew that was impossible.

'Shoot the damn horse!' Joey Franks shouted across to his companion. 'Just bring both of them down.'

The two outlaws fanned the hammers of their Colts. They had been trying to aim their shots at the rider, who was bent down behind the neck of the charging stallion, but knew that even though they were marksmen, it was a shot that nobody could make accurately.

The sheer momentum of the falling horse was a terrifying sight. As the noise of their pistols resounded all around them, the two men dived for cover. The sound of the huge animal's pitiful whinnying filled their ears for a fraction of a second before the creature crashed heavily into the dry undergrowth.

Franks had been hit by one of the stallion's shoulders and had been sent cartwheeling into the dense, brittle brush. For several minutes the outlaw was too dazed to move, then he rolled over. It took every ounce of his strength to pull himself free of the entangled branches that seemed to tear at his clothing like barbed wire.

As the cut and bleeding outlaw clawed his way to the huge grunting animal which lay on its side, Franks's eyes darted around, looking for the missing rider.

There was no sign of him.

Franks rubbed the blood from his face and then

realized that he had lost the pistol he had been hold-ing. His scratched left hand searched for his other .45. He sighed with relief as his fingers located the gun-grip in his holster.

His thumbnail flicked the leather loop off the gun hammer and he pulled the weapon free of its holster. With every movement his eyes darted around the scene, searching for the man whom he knew must be close.

Probably too close.

Dust still swirled in the moonlight as the outlaw tried to locate Red Clyde and the mysterious rider who had somehow vanished.

'Red. Where the hell are you?' Franks called out. There was no reply.

He attempted to listen for anything in the vicin-ity that might give him a clue as to what was going on. But the fallen horse was still noisily defying its own death and Joey Franks could hear nothing else.

Franks rested a hand on the nose of the stallion and tried to soothe its pain by stroking it. Then his attention was drawn to the rear legs of the powerful horse. For a moment the outlaw found himself smil-ing. He swallowed hard and moved carefully down the length of the fatally wounded animal until he reached the legs that protruded from beneath the stallion.

Then as he drew closer, his expression changed.

This was not the rider's legs, he thought. He recognized the spurs on the worn high-heeled boots.

120

Franks pulled back the hammer of his gun until it fully cocked.

This was Red Clyde!

NINETEEN

Dan Johnson had landed hard enough to knock every breath of wind from his body. He blinked hard and stared up at the brilliant moon directly above his head. A thousand war drums beat mercilessly inside his pounding skull as he realized that he was no longer galloping on the back of Mayor Martin's stallion. He wondered where he was and what had happened.

All the dazed rancher knew for sure was that he was somehow still alive.

Bruised, battered but alive.

His throbbing skull remembered seeing the two guns blasting at him as he had been thundering along the road. For a moment he tried to move and felt every bone in his body screaming in pain, yet nothing appeared to be broken. His hands checked his body until he was certain that none of the bullets had hit him.

Johnson turned his head slightly and looked over

to the left and then to the right. He could see nothing but bushes. He wondered where the horse had gone and then felt uncertain about the whereabouts of the outlaws.

They must be part of the ruthless gang who had displayed their deadly skills in and outside the Lucky Dime saloon. The rancher knew that he had to get up and away from this place before they homed in on him and finished him off.

But first he had to get his wind back. Sweat traced down his dust-covered temples and dripped on to the dry ground beside his head.

Where were the outlaws?

He was near the trail road but lying amid dry brush. Somehow the rancher forced himself up on to his elbows and then into a seated position. Dan Johnson sat silently trying to get his head to clear of the fog that swirled around his brain. Then a panic overwhelmed him.

His gun!

Where was his gun?

His hand moved frantically to the holster and found the pistol still there, held in place by the leather safety loop. He sighed with relief.

Johnson checked himself again for broken bones and then heard, coming from behind him, the pathetic whinnying of the stallion. For the first time since he had regained his senses, Johnson knew that at least two men had tried to kill him.

The lean man rolled on to his side and stared directly into the brush ahead of him. He could hear,

124

ahead of him, the spine-chilling noise of the dying horse. Johnson slid the pistol from his holster. His hand was trembling as he pulled the hammer back until it locked fully into place.

Where were they?

It had been years since Dan Johnson had last fired a handgun. He wondered if his skill would still be as good as it had once been.

He doubted it. There had been too many back-breaking years in between. Too many blistered hands and torn sinews.

He crawled towards the horrific sound.

Then Johnson's blood froze as he heard boots crushing the dried underbrush directly ahead of him.

Dan Johnson stopped crawling and watched as the boots appeared less than a yard in front of his face. Only a few branches separated them. The rancher stared at the boots as they moved on to the dusty road. Tilting his head, he could see Joey Franks searching for him with his lethal Colt .45 clutched in his right hand.

He looked every inch the outlaw.

Johnson rolled sideways and felt himself slipping down into a shallow trench. As he steadied himself and rose on to his knees, the rancher saw Franks spin around on his heels and fan his gun hammer.

He had heard the breaking branches!

A bullet snapped a branch off a few inches above Johnson's head.

Johnson was startled. He raised his gun and then felt the heat of another bullet burning through his shirt sleeve. The sound deafened him a split second later. The weary rancher dropped his gun and felt the agonizing pain tearing through his forearm. Frantically his eyes searched for the weapon but he could not see anything in the shadows.

The rancher leapt sideways as two more shots ripped at the brittle brush.

Johnson found himself lying next to the huge fallen stallion. He stared into the animal's unseeing eyes, and then at the bullet holes that peppered it's carcass. He had discovered what had happened to Hec Martin's horse.

'I know where you are, mister!' Franks shouted.

Dan Johnson looked over the stallion's neck and swallowed hard as he watched the outlaw emptying the spent shells from his gun and then reloading. For the first time since leaving the bank's office Johnson wondered if he had bitten off more than he could chew.

Joey Franks could see the movement behind the saddle on the horse. He fired again and watched the man duck. The outlaw knew that he had to give Rafe Jarrow and Neddy time to make their way across the shimmering salt-flats. The longer this execution took, the closer the two men would get to Cooper's Plain.

The outlaw began to move in on his target. It was obvious that the man in the ditch was unarmed or he

126

would have returned fire by this time.

This was going to be easy!

Dan Johnson stared down at his right arm. His sleeve was soaked in blood. The rancher flexed his fingers and felt the burning pain in his forearm. He checked it quickly. The bullet was lodged in the muscle but had not broken any bones. He rubbed his knuckles across his teeth and listened to the outlaw taunting him as he got closer.

'Show yourself ! Are you yella?' Franks laughed as he sent another bullet over the kneeling man's head.

Johnson saw Red Clyde's legs protruding from beneath the horse's body. He lay flat on his belly trying desperately to reach the dead man's gun belt. The horse was too heavy, though, and he had to admit defeat. There was no way he could prise the huge stallion's body off the dead outlaw.

The rancher rose to his knees again and peered over the horse's neck defiantly. This time he saw Franks's reaction and lowered his head a fraction of a second before the bullets were fired at him. Lumps of flesh were torn from the dead animal's body, showering the rancher in gore.

It was obvious that Joey Franks was no longer toying with him. Now he wanted another notch on his gun grip.

Johnson knew his time was running out. He looked to either side of him, but the thin, dry brush offered no cover in the bright moonlight. Behind him was the vast seemingly endless, salt-flats. They were not in a place a man would choose to visit willingly.

Then he spotted the two men and the horses walking out on the glistening white surface and was puzzled.

Who were they?

Where were they going?

Dan Johnson recalled Ed the bartender telling him about the outlaw named Rafe Jarrow and how he knew the mysterious Miss Candice. It suddenly dawned on Johnson: the two men were heading back to town.

Another bullet passed over his head and made Dan Johnson concentrate on the other outlaw, now relentlessly closing in on him.

He could hear Franks's footsteps.

The outlaw was too damn close!

Dan Johnson had nowhere to go and nothing with which to fend off his attacker. He pressed himself up close to the horse, then remembered the brand-new Winchester tucked into the cinch strap of the saddle. He closed his eyes and silently prayed that the animal was not lying on the rifle.

He swung around on his knees and saw the wooden rifle-stock jutting out from the saddle. Johnson tried to reach out for it but Franks fired again. The bullet hit the thick padded leather cantle and veered off into the brush.

Johnson knew that he had to distract the outlaw for a few seconds if he were to have a chance of reaching the fully loaded Winchester and extracting

128

it from its scabbard. He looked down at the two boots sticking out from beneath the dead stallion's belly.

Without a second thought, his fingers undid Red Clyde's spurs.

Johnson took a deep breath and then tossed the spurs over his head into the air. He prayed that they would land behind the outlaw.

They did!

He heard Joey Franks's boots turning on the dry ground as he looked to see what had made the sound that had just come from behind him.

Dan Johnson jumped to his feet and hauled the long-barrelled carbine from its scabbard and cranked its mechanism. The sound alerted the outlaw.

Joey Franks turned back to face the rancher.

Both men squeezed their triggers at exactly the same time, but it was Johnson who felt the kick of his Winchester in his hands as Franks's hammer fell on a spent bullet.

The rifle bullet blasted the outlaw off his feet. Joey Franks was thrown ten feet backwards, still clutching on to his empty Colt .45. He landed squarely on his back. A cloud of dust rose into the moonlight.

Dan Johnson staggered up from the brush behind the body of the horse and cocked the rifle again as he walked toward Franks.

Even in the eerie light of the moon, it was perfectly clear that the young outlaw was dead.

129

The rancher stared down at the dead man, who seemed to be frozen in death. His hand still held on to the Colt although it was aimed at the stars.

Johnson pulled the pistol from the lifeless hand and opened its smoking chamber. He emptied the shells out, then pulled bullets from his own gun belt to replace them as he walked towards the edge of the salt-flats.

His eyes narrowed, focusing on the two men with the four horses. They were at least a half-mile ahead of him. He knew that he could have picked them off with his rifle, but he was no back-shooter.

For a moment he thought about the outlaws' destination. The lights of Cooper's Plain twinkled in the moonlight away in the distance. Johnson wondered why they would return to a place which had already cost them so dearly. Then he thought about the saddle-bags on the backs of the horses they were leading. Bags filled with the golden coins that Braddock and Martin were so desperate to retrieve.

Dan Johnson returned to the dead horse and removed two of the full canteens from the saddle horn. He looped their long leather straps over his shoulders. He holstered Joey Franks's .45 and clasped the Winchester across his chest.

Then he walked out on to the salt-flats and followed the two outlaws. The ground felt strange beneath his boots. It gave way with the weight of each step. But he continued to follow.

One way or another, Dan Johnson was determined that he was going to catch up with these men.

TWENTY

The pursued and the pursuer had been walking over the salt-flats for more than two hours. The outlaws had not had a drop to drink since they had fled from the small town, unlike their relentless pursuer a half-mile behind on their tracks.

Although severely wounded and still losing blood, Rafe Jarrow had a gritty determination to reach Cooper's Plain and his beloved Miss Candice. It seemed that the further he walked, the more his mind drifted to thoughts of her.

The outlaw had known that he and Neddy Holmes were being trailed across the salt-flats by a man who must have somehow got the better of Red Clyde and Joey Franks.

To do so, this man was either an extremely good shot or very, very lucky. Jarrow was too weak to try and figure out which.

Whoever the man behind them was, Jarrow surmised, he seemed to be satisfied to maintain the distance between them. Never once trying to get closer. Confident enough to bide his time and strike when it suited him and not them.

The wounded leader of the once-famed Outfit was correct. Dan Johnson did not want to get too close to them and their lethal carbines. He just followed and watched as they got closer and closer to the small, unsuspecting town.

How Jarrow was still alive, let alone conscious, defied logic and yet the older outlaw still managed to keep pace with the much younger Holmes.

Jarrow just kept walking on towards Cooper's Plain.

Neddy Holmes seemed to be more agitated by the man who was following them. Every few yards, the outlaw would pause and look back at the figure illuminated by the moonlight, tracking them across the salt-flats.

'Who is he, Rafe?' Neddy asked for the umpteenth time. Jarrow continued walking with the reins of two horses in his weakening grip.

'How many times have I gotta answer that dumb-ass question, boy?' the grim-faced outlaw sighed.

Neddy Holmes dropped the reins of the horses and pulled his Winchester from the saddle scabbard. He cranked its well-oiled mechanism.

'I'm gonna end this,' he shouted, hoisting the rifle to his shoulder.

Jarrow looked over his shoulder at the hot-headed youngster and yelled at him:

'You fire that rifle and them horses are gonna spook, Neddy!'

134

Holmes felt a cold shiver tracing his spine. He knew that his wounded mentor was right. He was always right. Even half dead, he was still right. Holmes threw the rifle angrily to the ground and dropped to his knees, beating the salty surface with clenched fists.

'How can you keep so damn calm, Rafe? We've lost all our men and there's some dude dogging our tails and you still don't get worried.'

'I'm worried all right, Neddy,' Jarrow admitted for the first time since he had been wounded. 'I'm worried about not living much longer if'n I keep losing blood like this. I'm worried that we ain't gonna get us a chance to spend any of this gold. I'm even worried that we might never get back to the badlands. Hell, I reckon I must be the most worried critter in Texas right about now.'

Holmes turned and looked up at the outlaw, who was holding on to one of the saddles just to keep upright. He had never seen the man looking like this before. The light of the moon made Jarrow's features appear almost ghostlike.

'You look real bad, Rafe.' There was concern in the youngster's voice.

Jarrow managed to smile. Then he stared out at the figure who was defiantly trailing them. The expression soon changed to one of trepidation.

'You're right. He ain't gonna quit coming unless we stop him, Neddy.'

Holmes scrambled up off his knees and staggered back to Jarrow's side. Jarrow's eyes were now dark

135

through loss of blood and lack of water.

'You're dead right, Rafe. We gotta kill the bastard while we have the chance. We don't want that *hombre* following us into the town. He'll bring what's left of them townsfolk down on us, for sure.'

Jarrow felt the hand on his arm. He looked into the crazed eyes of the younger man. Eyes that he had never truly trusted in all the years they had ridden together.

'How do you figure on killing him, son?'

It was a simple question but its answer was far more complicated. Holmes looked at the figure of Dan Johnson and tried to swallow.

'Wish we had us a canteen of water, Rafe,' he said, stepping away from the older man and screwing up his eyes. He gazed into the shimmering heat haze, which was still rising from the vast desert of salt almost three and a half hours after the sun had set. 'I ain't gonna let that man kill us like he must have killed Red and Joey.'

'Damn right,' Jarrow agreed.

'But it gotta be done right. We gotta figure out the best way of putting him out of his misery.' There was a smile on the cracked lips of the outlaw.

'You could stay here and wait for him to come into range,' Rafe Jarrow suggested.

Neddy Holmes nodded, then looked over his shoulder.

'Or I could mount one of the horses and ride straight down his throat, Rafe.'

Jarrow nodded. He was too weak to think straight any longer.

'Yep. Either way you'll kill the critter.'

Neddy Holmes scooped his rifle up from the ground and blew the salt from it. He picked up the reins to one of the animals and handed them to Jarrow. Then he turned to the unscathed horse, grabbed hold of the saddle horn and stepped into the stirrup. He mounted the horse and steadied it.

Jarrow watched as the younger man turned the horse around to face the approaching Johnson. He checked the carbine and laid it across his lap.

'You figure that this man is a good shot, Neddy?'

Holmes tried to lick his lips but had no spittle. 'I'll have to make sure I'm a tad more accurate than him. Right?'

Jarrow nodded, gathered up the reins of the three horses in his hands and headed once more for Cooper's Plains.

'Right, Neddy.'

Neddy Holmes's eyes screwed right up as he looked at the distant figure.

'He's a dead man, Rafe.' He laughed.

Rafe Jarrow watched the rider spurring his mount and heading off towards Dan Johnson. The horse seemed unable to make any pace on the unstable surface. It staggered with every other stride, but Holmes continued to jab his spurs into the animal's flesh.

'Best of luck, Neddy. You'll need it.'

Dan Johnson had continued to head straight at the men and their horses, even though he had seen them stopping to look at him. He paused only when

137

he had spotted one of the outlaws mounting one of the horses. Johnson unscrewed the stopper from the neck of one of his canteens and took a long swallow of the refreshing water.

He watched as the rider headed directly for him, but felt no fear. For some reason the outlaw imagined that he had an advantage by being on horseback.

Dan Johnson knelt on the salty ground and raised his Winchester to his shoulder. He closed one eye as he stared down the long barrel and focused through the sights.

It was obvious to Johnson that the horseman had no knowledge of this dangerous land, otherwise he would never have risked getting on to the back of his horse and attempting to ride over the salt surface.

Johnson licked his thumb and wetted the further sight before placing his index finger on the trigger.

He watched Neddy Holmes raise his own rifle and fire. The bullet missed by a dozen yards. The horse's hoofs were not suited for the salt-flats, neither was its weight.

Johnson remained exactly where he was and waited for the rider to get well within range. The horse stumbled and then had to be dragged up by its reins to prevent it from falling into the shifting surface of the salt flat.

Neddy Holmes somehow managed to crank the mechanism of his Winchester again as he bore down on the kneeling rancher. This time the bullet came within a few yards of its target.

Dan Johnson squeezed the trigger gently and felt the rifle kick in his shoulder. The horse reared up and bucked out at the stars as its master rolled backwards off the saddle and fell heavily into the salty ground. Neddy Holmes rolled on to his side, drew one of his pistols and fired.

The bullet passed within inches of the rancher's face. He felt the heat of the bullet on his cheek.

Holmes pulled back his gun hammer once more with his thumbs. Johnson heard it click into position.

The rancher rose to his feet and cranked the rifle again. He fired. This time his bullet found its mark. The young outlaw died instantly. Dan Johnson strode over the ground and looked at the body. Then he looked towards the distant Rafe Jarrow, who had almost reached the sleeping town.

Johnson glanced at the confused horse, and then at the loaded bags tied to the saddle cantle.

He began walking again after Jarrow.

This time his pace was much faster.

TWENTY-ONE

More dead than alive, Rafe Jarrow led the three horses off the salt-flats and somehow managed to continue walking through the dry brush towards the first of the wooden buildings which, collectively, had become known as Cooper's Plain.

A few paces into the sparse undergrowth the outlaw paused and looked back at the desert of white, glistening salt. Dan Johnson was still following him.

Who was he? Jarrow wondered angrily. Was he one of the deputies? That seemed impossible. They had been totally out of their depth even with loaded rifles in their hands. They had claimed the lives of two of his best men but that had been more by luck than skill. Even a drunkard can hit a man if he aims at a crowd, the outlaw fumed.

Whoever it was who was out there on the salt flats, he had been gaining ground steadily since he had dispatched the haplass Neddy Holmes. Jarrow had always known that the young outlaw's lack of accuracy would one day be the ruin of him.

Johnson was now almost running across the salty ground after the outlaw. Jarrow knew that he had to act quickly if he were to have even the remotest chance of surviving until dawn, yet he could not risk firing at his hunter. This would alert the entire township.

Without his Outfit to back him up, Jarrow knew he had to be cautious. Cautious or dead.

He pulled the golden watch from his vest pocket. It was covered in blood. He wiped it on his sleeve and then opened the cover. It was nearly ten. Early enough for there to be people still wide awake, the outlaw thought.

Jarrow gritted his teeth and touched his side for the hundredth time. Then he looked at the blood on his fingertips and inhaled deeply as he returned the hunter to the blood-soaked pocket.

Jarrow knew that he needed a doctor or harness-maker to sew him up and stop the relentless loss of blood. But there was no time for such things. He jerked the reins and led the three horses round to the back of the buildings, towards his goal.

The Lucky Dime saloon was less than 500 yards away, but every step was now becoming torturous.

When he reached the rear of the saloon Jarrow paused and tied all three horses to a wooden upright. It was not the best place to leave the fortune that filled the leather satchels of his saddle-bags, but he was too weak even to think of trying to get them inside the building.

Just as the outlaw was about to move away from the horses, a drunken man staggered from the rear door and made for the saloon's outhouse.

The man looked up at Jarrow, then stopped walking. He pushed his Stetson up on to his brow and squinted at the face of the infamous outlaw.

'Have we ever met, stranger?' The drunk asked, looking at the outhouse.

Jarrow forced a smile and nodded, moving away from the three horses and closer to the man, who was now unbuttoning his trousers.

'Nope, and we never will again,' Jarrow said coldly.

Before the drunken man could reply he felt the knife thrusting up beneath his ribs. The pain tore through him but the outlaw's hand muffled any cries he might have been capable of making. Rafe Jarrow withdrew the blade from the man and wiped it on his sleeve before sliding it back into his boot. The man landed at his feet with the shocked expression carved into his features that Jarrow had witnessed countless times before.

Jarrow pushed the body beneath the saloon porch and straightened up. He had never felt such agony before, but still he would not even consider quitting. He had to get back to Miss Candice and explain that he had not broken his promise to her earlier that afternoon. It seemed to be the only

143

thought left in his fog-filled mind.

His eyes narrowed as he stared down the dark alley. Men were still walking up and down the main street, totally unaware that their worst nightmare had returned into their midst. A man who was capable of killing for the sheer pleasure of it.

Rafe Jarrow drew one of his guns and stepped on to the rear porch of the wooden building. He turned the handle of the door and pushed it open. The outlaw knew that the only way to Miss Candice's room was through the saloon. It was not a route he would have chosen willingly.

He entered and made his way into the darkness.

Jarrow stopped beside the door that led into the saloon. The very door that the four rifle-toting deputies had used when catching him and his gang in a crossfire earlier that same day. His cold lifeless eyes studied the bullet holes that had torn the door to shreds.

The injured outlaw pulled the door ajar and peered into the room. There were two men drinking at the bar and another three playing poker at a table.

He tried to swallow but his throat was too dry. He yearned for something to drink. Anything at all.

Without even pausing to consider the possible consequences, Jarrow pulled the door open and walked into the room. The stench of spent bullets still lingered in the stale air of the smoke-filled room, but the outlaw ignored it. He kept the gun held

144

firmly in his hand and walked through the sawdust towards the staircase.

It was only thirty feet away to the first of the fifteen steps but to his tired legs it seemed more like a hundred miles. It took every ounce of his dwindling willpower just to put one foot in front of another.

With each carefully placed step, his eyes stared down at the bare floorboards which still bore the stains of the earlier blood-bath, which no amount of scrubbing had been able to remove. He reached the foot of the stairs and was about to start the short climb back to the arms of the fragile, dying woman when he heard the unmistakable voice of the bartender behind him.

'Where the hell do you think you're going, mister?' Ed called out. All eyes stared at the dishevelled figure.

Rafe Jarrow hesitated for a few seconds, then he continued to climb the steps back to the room where he had last seen the once-beautiful woman.

Ed the bartender walked from behind the bar and through the freshly laid sawdust towards him but Jarrow continued to climb the wooden steps.

'You can't go up there, stranger!'

Rafe Jarrow pulled the pistol across his waist so that the men in the saloon would not see it and get the wrong idea of what his mission really was. He did not want them to think that he was someone intent on hurting the mysterious Candice LeBeau.

'Hey, mister! Are you deaf or something? Them's

145

private quarters up there. Nobody can go up there without permission of Miss Candice.'

'I know,' Jarrow said as his weak legs reached the landing and halted. He kept his back to the bartender who was walking up the threadbare stair carpet behind him. The outlaw knocked on the door just as Ed reached the landing and stepped up behind the blood-soaked outlaw.

'Who is it?' The frail voice called out.

'It's Rafe, Candice. I've returned.'

The bartender froze behind the outlaw and began to shake. Now he recognized the clothes of the man before him but the last time he had seen them they were not drenched in blood.

'Come in, Rafe. It's not locked,' Miss Candice's voice said to the man she had believed she would never see again.

Jarrow tilted his head and glanced into the eyes of the bartender, who was standing open-mouthed at the top of the stairs.

'There are three horses tied up out back, barkeep,' Jarrow said, tossing two golden eagles into the man's sweating hands. 'Bring the saddle-bags up here.'

'Anything else?'

'Yeah. You ain't seen me!'

Ed watched Jarrow enter the room.

'I ain't seen nobody!' The bartender nodded.

TWENTY-TWO

The bartender's fingers worked on the leather laces
that held the last of the saddle-bags on the back of
the third horse. He hauled the heavy satchel of
golden coins from behind the cantle and dropped it
at his feet next to the others. For a few moments he
just stood gasping for air as he wondered how much
money was actually inside these innocent-looking
bags.

He heard footsteps coming from behind him and
slowly turned to face Dan Johnson. Even in the
moonlight he could see that he too was wounded.
The man's right sleeve was soaked in blood.

'You gave me a fright, Dan,' Ed said shaking his
head and rubbing the palms of his hands on his
white shirt.

Johnson said nothing. He looked into the shadows
of the alley and then at the open doorway to the rear
of the Lucky Dime. Only then did he lower the
Winchester.

'You're wounded!' the bartender said, trying to

147

hide the swollen saddle-bags behind his painfully thin legs.

'Yep. I caught me a bullet,' the rancher said, moving cautiously around the three horses.

'You ought to get that tended, Dan.'

Johnson looked down.

'What's in the bags, Ed?'

There was a long silence. The bartender did not know what to do for the best. Should he tell Dan Johnson the truth and risk the life of his employer? Or should he try to bluff his way out of this? Neither sat well with the man who had never done anything more dangerous than once opening a bottle of French wine.

'What are you doing here, Dan?'

Johnson stepped closer to the man. He watched the beads of sweat trickling down the man's face and then nodded. Ed was a loyal man.

'Is Miss Candice OK?'

'Yep. Why?' Ed was confused.

'She got company?'

The bartender went silent once more.

Dan Johnson bent down and opened one of the saddle-bags' leather flaps. The light of the large moon danced over the golden coins.

'This money was stolen from the noon stage, Ed.'

The man looked down sheepishly and blinked hard when he too focused on the coins.

'Look at all that gold. I never seen so much gold.'

'Me neither, Ed.' Johnson stepped up on to the boardwalk and stared down the dark corridor that

148

led to the heart of the saloon. 'Where is he?'

'This is darn awkward for me, Dan,' Ed said.

'I know.' Johnson unscrewed the stopper to one of his canteens and took a long swallow. 'Those outlaws were all killers and there's just one of the varmints left. And he's somewhere inside the Lucky Dime. I've gotta finish this, Ed.'

'Why? You ain't no lawman or bounty hunter.' The bartender was getting agitated and it showed.

Johnson could not understand why.

'What's eating at you?'

'Nothing! I just don't see why you are so damn intent on killing Rafe Jarrow, Dan. Why? You ain't no gunfighter. You're just a rancher like most of the folks around here. Why are you so all fired-up?'

'I ain't. I just agreed that I'd get the money from the stagecoach robbery back to old man Braddock.' Johnson rubbed his forearm. The bullet beneath his skin was throbbing with every beat of his heart.

'Then how come you're so darn interested if that outlaw is inside the saloon?'

'Because I intend to stop that man from hurting anyone ever again, Ed.' Johnson cranked the Winchester. The memory of all the dead and wounded men filled his tired mind.

Ed placed a hand on the shoulder of the rancher.

'You don't understand, Dan. They're both up there now in her room. Both as close to death as it's probably possible to get without actually being nailed down in a wooden box.'

Dan Johnson expression altered.

149

'What ya mean?'

'I ain't supposed to know nothing but I knows a lot. Miss Candice is dying, Dan. She ain't bin able to eat no food now for the longest of times. She thinks I'm too dumb to figure out why she hides away up there keeping her face away from me when I takes her up her mint tea. But I know when someone is headed for boot hill.'

Johnson rubbed his jaw.

'She's dying? How?'

'The cancer, Dan.' There were tears in the loyal man's eyes as he spoke. 'I seen her reflection in the mirror a week or so back. Her face is being eaten away. It's all black on the one side. She's a goner.'

Dan Johnson knew that death wore many masks. He had seen most of them over the last six months.

'And Rafe Jarrow?'

'He's shot through, Dan. That man can't have more than a thimbleful of blood left in his entire body.'

'Why did he come back?'

'He run out on her once. Maybe he just wants to die with her, Dan.' The bartender rubbed his eyes on his shirt sleeve.

The rancher stared down at the saddlebags and shook his head.

'What were you intending to do with them bags, Ed?'

'Jarrow told me to bring them up to him.'

Johnson reached down and lifted one of the hefty bags.

150

'Then that's exactly what you're gonna do. I'll help you.'

The two men carried the bags through the rear of the saloon into the brightly illuminated interior of the Lucky Dime. Dan Johnson knew that Ed had spoken the truth about Jarrow's condition when his keen eyes spotted the trail of blood on the fresh sawdust at their feet.

It led straight up the worn carpeting on the staircase to the landing. The rancher paused and gazed at the door that he knew led to the room occupied by the once beautiful Candice LeBeau.

'You ought to leave them be, Dan,' Ed said in a low voice that was for Johnson's ears only.

Dan Johnson was about to speak when he saw the banker and the town mayor enter through what remained of the swing doors.

'Johnson!' Braddock boomed loudly across the saloon. He marched up to the tall lean figure. 'What you doing here in the saloon? I paid you to go looking for them stagecoach robbing swine.'

Dan Johnson squared up to the noisy banker.

'I've just gotten back, Mr Braddock.'

'I didn't see my stallion outside, Dan. Where is he?'

'I'm sorry, Mr Mayor. Your horse got shot out from under me on the Smith's Spring road.'

Cecil Braddock's eyes locked on to the three bulging leather bags in the two men's arms.

'What's in them saddle-bags, Dan?'

'The strongbox money, I reckon,' the rancher

replied honestly. The banker suddenly smiled.

'You managed to get the money back? Bravo, young man. Bravo!'

'You killed all them outlaws?' Hec Martin asked.

Johnson shook his head.

'Not all of them, Mr Mayor. One got away.'

'So one of the bastards got away. What does it matter? We have our money back. That's all that really matters.' Braddock could not seem to keep the volume of his voice down. He grabbed one of the bags from the bartender, placed it on top of a card-table and unbuckled it. His eyes widened as he looked at the glistening coins.

'Bring my money on up here!' Rafe Jarrow's voice cut through the air within the Lucky Dime saloon like a lightning bolt.

Dan Johnson's eyes were the first to lock on to the gruesome sight of the blood-soaked outlaw. Within seconds everyone else had also focused on the grim figure standing like a ghost at the top of the stairs.

Braddock's head turned to the rancher.

'What's going on here, Dan?' he shouted.

Johnson did not take his eyes off the outlaw as he replied to the banker.

'That's Rafe Jarrow, Mr Braddock. He's the outlaw that I was telling you about. The one that ain't dead yet.'

Using every ounce of what remained of her once boundless courage, Miss Candice LeBeau walked from her room and out on to the landing. She stood next to the man she still loved.

A huge gasp of shock went around the room as the men inside her saloon gazed up at her in disbelief. She had pushed her long hair off her face and allowed them all to see the black, deformed features.

'You heard me! Bring them bags up to me!' Jarrow growled as his hands toyed with the grips of his deadly Colts.

Braddock cleared his throat and pointed at the two figures.

'This is bank money. You have no claim on it.'

Jarrow was in no mood to argue. Somehow he took a step forward and defiantly pointed a finger down at the banker.

'I'll kill you first if them bags ain't brought up here in five seconds.'

Braddock glanced at Martin and nodded. 'Get him, Hec!'

The mayor drew his own pistol and fired shots at the outlaw. Bullets tore through the stale air from Martin's Colt as the mayor moved closer to the foot of the stairs. He only stopped squeezing his trigger when his gun was empty.

When the acrid gunsmoke cleared, the men within the saloon saw that the once beautiful Miss Candice was being cradled in the arms of the kneeling Rafe Jarrow. Dan Johnson dropped the saddlebags to the floor, and tore the gun from Martin's hand and tossed it the length of the long room.

'You damn fool,' the rancher snarled. 'You killed her. You killed Miss Candice.'

There was a hushed silence within the room.

153

The mayor stepped back to the side of the banker as if trying to seek protection from his associate. Braddock pulled his own pistol from his holster and cocked its hammer.

Slowly Rafe Jarrow lowered the lifeless body of his beloved Candice on to the floor. She had used herself as a shield and taken every bullet intended for him. The outlaw lifted her red hair and draped it over her face to hide the black cancerous growth. Slowly he straightened up and glared down at the two men huddled together.

At that same moment Sheriff Jake Walker staggered into the saloon, having slept off his drink. He saw Jarrow descending the stairs with his hands on his gun grips. The outlaw stopped and looked over the heads of the banker and the mayor at the lawman.

'That's Rafe Jarrow of the Outfit, men,' Walker cried out, drawing his own weapons.

Without a moment's hesitation, Jarrow drew his guns and placed two bullets into the chests of both Martin and Braddock. Then, looking up, he aimed his weapons at Walker and smiled.

Before the two men had hit the sawdust, a shot echoed around the interior of the Lucky Dime.

Jarrow fell forward and rolled down the remaining wooden steps of the staircase. He ended up at the feet of Dan Johnson and lay open-eyed, staring at the rancher.

Johnson knelt down and took the pistols from the man's bloody hands and checked them. The cham-

154

bers of both Colts were filled with spent shells.

'Are you the man who was trailing us out there on the salt-flats?' Jarrow asked, blood running from the corner of his mouth.

'Yep,' Johnson replied. He placed the guns on the floor.

'You did good.'

Johnson glanced across at the dead banker and mayor. He felt no pity.

'Did you know these guns were empty when you trained them on the sheriff?'

Jarrow smiled. 'Sure did.'

Dan Johnson felt a cold shiver trace his spine when the outlaw's head rolled over for the last time. He rose to his feet, walked slowly through the gathered crowd and out of the building.

At least Jarrow was now with his woman, he thought. Unlike himself.

FINALE

The stagecoach had eventually continued on its journey to the next town with the wily old Sagebrush sitting high on the driver's seat, but there had been no passengers. Dan Johnson was curious about that as he sat on a barrel outside the livery stable and thoughtfully stared out at the new day as the sun began to rise above Cooper's Plain.

Where was the handsome woman whose modesty he had gallantly salvaged?

The sound of footsteps drew Johnson's attention. Gus Dekker ran his large fingers through his thinning hair and yawned as he walked out of the livery stable towards the rancher.

'You want some breakfast, Dan?'

Johnson nodded. 'Sure. I could use some good cooking.'

The livery owner stared at his friend's bandaged arm and rested a boot on a fence pole.

'Did you let the doc cut that bullet out, Dan?'

Johnson stood and stared at his arm. It no longer hurt.

'Yep. Reckon I felt sorry for him. He ain't had too many patients who are still breathing over the last twenty-four hours.'

'What you thinking about?' Dekker asked.

Johnson turned and looked at the big man.

'I asked Jake Walker a question this morning.'

'What kinda question?'

'I asked him who owns a horse whose master has been killed.'

Dekker rubbed his chin. It seemed a strange question to ask anyone, let alone their sheriff.

'Did our young sheriff know the answer?'

'Yep. He said that if a man gets himself killed, his horse and its saddle and tack belongs to whoever catches the critter. If'n the dead man ain't got no kin, that is.' Johnson leaned on the top fence pole and stared into the corral. 'Ain't that interesting?'

Dekker scratched his head.

'Is it? That sounds about right but how come you asked him a question like that in the first place, Dan?'

Dan Johnson smiled.

'It is interesting if you know that there just happens to be a horse out there on the salt-flats whose master is lying stone dead.'

'And you need a horse?' Dekker came to stand beside the rancher.

Johnson shrugged. 'Not really, but one with a saddle-bag on its back filled with golden eagles might

158

have its uses, Gus.'

The livery owner placed a hand on the lean shoulder.

'I thought that Jake Walker had all the bank's gold safely locked up, Dan?'

Dan Johnson sighed. 'So does he.'

'You mean that there was a fourth bag of coins?' Dekker raised his eyebrows. 'One that nobody seems to know about?'

'Yep. What do you figure the reward for finding that bag would be, Gus? Ten per cent?'

The large man rubbed his hands together eagerly. 'It sounds like we might make us a few bucks, Dan.'

'Do you feel like taking a buckboard ride down the trail road so that we can see if that horse is still out there on the salt-flats?'

'I'll hitch up a team, Dan.'

Dan Johnson inhaled deeply. Then he noticed the handsome female stagecoach passenger whom he had helped the day before. She was going into a small café opposite. Without even knowing why, he walked across the wide street towards the café.

'I think I'll get me some breakfast over yonder, Gus,' Dan called out over his shoulder. 'You hitch up that team. I'll be back in a while.'

Gus Dekker grinned.

'Take ya time, Dan. Reckon that horse ain't going no place.'